AF289012

THE SUCCESSOR

BY:LEA LARSEN

TABLE OF CONTENTS:

Chapter One 5

Chapter Two..19

Chapter Three 49

Chapter Four 65

Chapter Five 79

Chapter Six 109

Chapter One

"COME ON PETE! LOOSEN UP!"

ANDI COOKE PUT HER HANDS ON HER COUSIN'S SHOULDERS AND SHOOK HIM PLAYFULLY AS THOUGH SHE WAS TRYING TO DISLODGE A LONG STICK THAT HAD BEEN STUCK INSIDE HIS RECTUM. AND, AS SHE REMINDED HERSELF, THAT WASN'T FAR FROM WHAT SHE WAS TRYING TO DO.

HER COUSIN PETER HAD BEEN SITTING AT THE END OF THE BAR ALL NIGHT STILL NURSING, FROM WHAT ANDI COULD TELL, HIS VERY FIRST DRINK. A MILLER LIGHT BEER.

"I THINK I'LL STICK TO THE BAR, THANKS," HE SAID.

ANDI PUT HER HANDS ON HER HIPS AND GAVE HIM A LIGHT GLARE.

"WHY DID YOU BRING ME ALL THE WAY FROM TEXAS TO MASSACHUSETTS THIS SUMMER SO WE COULD "HANG OUT" IF YOU WERE GOING TO SPEND THE WHOLE TIME MOPING?"

"I'M NOT MOPING," PETER SAID. "I'M

STAYING HERE BECAUSE IT'S EASIER TO SPOT TROUBLE FROM THIS VANTAGE POINT."

"WHAT TROUBLE COULD WE POSSIBLY GET INTO?" ANDI ASKED. IT WASN'T A LARGE CLUB, AFTER ALL. AND, SALEM MASSACHUSETTS, AS FAR AS SHE KNEW, WAS GENERALLY A PRETTY SAFE SMALL CITY.

"THE MORE GUYS YOU DANCE WITH, THE MORE TROUBLE THERE COULD BE," PETER SAID. THOUGH HIS VOICE WAS PROTECTIVE, SHE SAW A TEASING SMIRK ON HIS LIPS.

IT WAS TRUE, THE THREE WHITE RUSSIANS (SO FAR), THAT SHE HAD CONSUMED HAD CAUSED HER TO DANCE WITH MORE STRANGE MEN THAN MIGHT BE DEEMED PROPER. SHE'D EVEN KISSED ABOUT THREE OF THEM. STILL, IT WASN'T AS BAD AS IT COULD HAVE BEEN.

WHITE RUSSIANS, AFTER ALL, TENDED TO GO TO SKINNY GIRLS HEADS. LUCKILY, ANDI WAS NOT A SKINNY GIRL AND DIDN'T HAVE THAT PROBLEM.

ASIDE FROM PROVIDING HER WITH CURVES THAT, WHILE NOT CONFORMING TO THE STICK THIN HOLLYWOOD STANDARD, LET HER SEE PLENTY OF ACTION FROM MORE OPEN MINDED AND INTERESTING MEN, HER WEIGHT ALSO ALLOWED HER TO HOLD HER DRINK WELL.

THAT NIGHT, SHE'D TAKEN FULL ADVANTAGE OF HER "SUPER POWER" AS SHE CALLED IT. THOUGH, SHE HAD, LUCKILY MANAGED TO LOOSE HER MAKE OUT PARTNERS IN THE CROWD.

MAKING OUT WITH GUYS AT A CLUB WAS ONE THING. BUT, SHE WOULD NEVER LOOK FOR A BOYFRIEND HERE. NOT EVEN A ONE NIGHT STAND. DESPITE HER LOVE OF DANCING AND A GOOD TIME, SHE DIDN'T LIKE MAKING DECISIONS ABOUT SEX WHEN SHE WAS LESS THAN SOBER.

BUT, NOW, HER COUSIN'S MOPING IN THE CORNER KEPT DRAWING HER ATTENTION FROM THE DANCE FLOOR. AND SHE'D FINALLY DECIDED IT WAS TIME TO DO SOMETHING ABOUT IT.

"COME ON," SHE SAID, GRABBING HOLD OF HIS ARM. "COME DANCE."

"REALLY ANDI, I'M OK HERE," HE SAID SHAKING OFF HER GRIP. "IN FACT, WE SHOULD PROBABLY GO SOON."

"WHAT DO YOU MEAN?" SHE ASKED. "IT'S ONLY MIDNIGHT! PARTY'S JUST STARTING!"

"I'VE HEARD THAT MIDNIGHT IS WHEN THINGS START TO GET ROUGH," PETE SAID. ANDI ROLLED HER EYES.

"WELL, IT DOESN'T LOOK LIKE YOUR FRIENDS WANT TO GO ANYTIME SOON," SHE SAID. ANDI NODDED AND BROUGHT PETE'S ATTENTION TO THE TWO MEN A LITTLE WAYS IN FRONT OF THEM.

THEY WERE PETE'S FRIENDS FROM COLLEGE. BROTHERS, THOUGH YOU WOULD NEVER KNOW IT. THE YOUNGEST, CAIN, WAS RUDDY FACED WITH BROWN CURLY HAIR AND WARM HAZEL EYES. HE WAS SHORT AND FAIRLY STOCKY.

HE SEEMED TO BE LAUGHING AS A BEAUTIFUL, THIN BLONDE GIRL, CLEARLY DRUNK, MOVED HER HIPS CONTINUALLY AGAINST HIM.

HIS OLDER BROTHER, SETH, SEEMED AT EASE THOUGH SLIGHTLY LESS ENTERTAINED THAN CAIN. HIS SKIN MORE CLOSELY RESEMBLED ANDI'S OWN FAIR COMPLEXION, THOUGH, TRUTH BE TOLD, HIS WAS NEARLY WHITE. HE HAD LIGHT GREY EYES AND DARK HAIR AS WELL AS A HEIGHT THAT MADE HIM STAND OUT.

HE STOOD ALONE A WAYS FROM THE DANCE FLOOR AND BOBBED HIS HEAD IN TIME WITH THE MUSIC. HE WAS ANOTHER ONE WHO LOOKED AS THOUGH HE COULD USE A GOOD SHAKE TO LOOSEN A STICK UP HIS BUTT. HE

LOOKED MORE THAN A LITTLE STIFF OUT THERE. STILL, UNLIKE PETE, AT LEAST HE WAS MAKING AN EFFORT.

NEXT TO ANDI, SHE HEARD PETE HEAVE A SIGH.

"FINE," HE SAID. "I GUESS WE CAN STAY FOR A BIT. BUT, YOU'RE NOT GOING TO GET ME TO DANCE."

ANDI ROLLED HER EYES AT HIM.

"WELL, THEN AT LEAST LET ME GET YOU ANOTHER DRINK. YOU'VE BEEN SIPPING ON THAT ONE ALL NIGHT."

"I'M NOT FINISHED WITH IT."

"SO, I'LL GET YOU ANOTHER ONE TO START ON WHEN YOU ARE FINISHED," SHE SAID. AND WITHOUT WAITING FOR HIS APPROVAL, SHE HOPPED OFF THE STOOL AND MADE HER WAY ACROSS THE BAR WHERE A HARASSED LOOKING BARTENDER WAS TAKING DRINK ORDERS FROM WHAT LOOKED LIKE A THIRSTY HORDE.

ANDI TRIED TO PUSH HER WAY THROUGH THEM INTENT ON GETTING PETE ANOTHER DRINK. MAYBE THAT WOULD LOOSEN HIM UP AND STOP ALL THIS SILLY TALK OF LEAVING EARLY.

SHE FELT HERSELF GETTING PULLED INTO THE CROWD. BEING ELBOWED AND SHOVED. SHE TRIED TO USE HER GIRTH AS WELL AS THE SKILLS SHE HAD LEARNED IN HER VARIOUS KICKBOXING CLASSES TO FIGHT HER WAY THROUGH BUT, TO NO AVAIL.

"HAVING TROUBLE," A SLOW AND AMUSED VOICE ASKED FROM BEHIND HER. SHE TURNED TO SEE SETH LOOKING AT HER A COCKY SMILE ON HIS LIPS.

"HOW COULD YOU TELL?" SHE ASKED DRYLY.

"MAYBE IT'S A SIGN," HE SAID.

"A SIGN OF WHAT?"

"THAT WE SHOULD HEAD OUT."

ANDI ROLLED HER EYES AGAIN AS SHE FELT A MIXTURE OF FRUSTRATION AND ANNOYANCE CREEP THROUGH HER.

"YOU SOUND LIKE PETE," SHE SAID. "SERIOUSLY, WHAT'S THE POINT OF GOING OUT IF WE'RE NOT STAYING UNTIL THE CLUB CLOSES?"

"SOME PEOPLE WOULD SAY IT'S BEST TO QUIT WHILE YOU'RE AHEAD."

SHE TURNED TO HIM AGAIN, THAT ANNOYINGLY SMUG SMILE WAS STILL ON HIS FACE. SHE DIDN'T THINK SHE'D EVER SEEN HIM WITH ANOTHER EXPRESSION. HE ALWAYS LOOKED EITHER BORED AND ARROGANT OR SMUG AND DOUCHEY.

OF COURSE, HE DID HAVE A SORT OF CASUAL ELEGANCE ABOUT HIM THAT, SHE SUPPOSED, WAS ATTRACTIVE. STILL, IT DIDN'T MAKE UP FOR BEING AN ARROGANT PRICK.

"WELL, I DON'T BELIEVE IN QUITTING," SHE SAID AND, WITH AN ENTIRELY FAKE, SARDONIC SMILE, SHE SHOVED HER WAY BACK INTO THE CROWD.

SHE'D JUST BEGUN THROWING A FEW ELBOWS OF HER OWN WHEN SHE HEARD A WELCOME VOICE CALL OUT FROM BEHIND THE BAR.

"I CAN TAKE AN ORDER OVER HERE," IT SAID.

SHE LOOKED UP TO SEE ANOTHER BARTENDER WHO NEITHER SHE NOR ANYONE ELSE AROUND HER HAD NOTICED BEFORE. HE WAS SHORT WITH BLACK CURLY HAIR AND A NICE OLIVE COMPLEXION.

GRATEFUL, SHE RUSHED TOWARDS THE

END OF THE BAR WHERE HE STOOD, HOPING THE CROWD WOULD NOT FOLLOW HER.

"A MILLER LIGHT AND A…"

"WHITE RUSSIAN?" HE ASKED BEFORE SHE COULD FINISH.

"HOW'D YOU KNOW?"

"THAT'S WHAT YOU'VE BEEN DRINKING ALL NIGHT ISN'T IT?" HE ASKED. HE FLASHED HER A SMILE MUCH MORE GENUINE AND A THOUSAND TIMES MORE WELCOME THAN THE ONE SHE'D JUST GOTTEN FROM SETH. SHE WAS SO DISARMED BY THE SPARKLE IN HIS EYES AND THE BLINDING WHITENESS OF HIS TEETH THAT SHE DIDN'T EVEN STOP TO THINK THAT HE COULDN'T HAVE KNOWN HER DRINK ORDER. SHE HADN'T SEEN HIM BEHIND THE BAR ALL EVENING.

"YEAH," SHE SAID. "AND SEND THE MILLER LIGHT DOWN TO THAT MOPEY LOOKING GUY AT THE END OF THE BAR."

SHE POINTED AT HER COUSIN WHO WAS STILL LOOKING AROUND THE CLUB, BEER IN HAND, SITTING AT THE EDGE OF HIS SEAT AS THOUGH WAITING FOR THE PLACE TO CATCH FIRE AT ANY MINUTE.

"I'VE GOT TO SAY," THE BARTENDER SAID

TURNING TO GRAB THE BEER. "IF I WERE HERE WITH A GIRL AS PRETTY AS YOU, I WOULDN'T BE SITTING AT THE BAR LOOKING GLOOMY."

ANDI LAUGHED. PARTLY AT THE THOUGHT THAT A GUY AS GOOD LOOKING AT THIS ONE HAD ACTUALLY CALLED HER PRETTY AND PARTLY AT THE IDEA THAT SHE AND PETE WERE AN ITEM.

"HE'S MY COUSIN," SHE SAID WITH A CHUCKLE. SHE ALSO FOUND HERSELF TOSSING HER LONG, DIRTY BLONDE HAIR FLIRTILY BEHIND HER AND PRAYING THAT A SENSUAL SPARKLE LIT HER GREEN EYES.

"SO, I TAKE IT YOU'RE NOT ATTACHED?" HE ASKED HANDING HER THE WHITE RUSSIAN SHE'D ORDERED.

"YOU COULD SAY THAT," SHE SAID LEANING OVER THE BAR AND GIVING HIM HER BRIGHTEST FLIRTY SMILE. "I'M JUST BABYSITTING MY COUSIN AND A COUPLE OF HIS FRIENDS TONIGHT."

"DO YOU THINK THEY'D MISS YOU IF YOU DIPPED OUT FOR A FEW MINUTES?" HE ASKED.

SHE TOOK A LONG SIP OF THE DRINK HE'D JUST HANDED HER, TRYING TO PIECE TOGETHER WHAT THIS GOOD LOOKING GUY HAD JUST ASKED HER. AND EVEN MORE

IMPORTANTLY, TRYING TO THINK OF WHAT SHE MIGHT SAY IN RESPONSE.

ANDI SET HER GLASS DOWN ON THE COUNTER, VAGUELY REALIZING THAT SHE MAY HAVE HAD A LITTLE TOO MUCH A LITTLE TOO FAST.

"DEPENDS," SHE TOLD THE BARTENDER FINALLY. SHE FELT A SLIGHTLY PLEASANT AND SLIGHTLY UNNERVING BUZZ IN HER HEAD.

"ON WHAT?" HE ASKED LEANING OVER THE BAR.

"ON WHO I DIP OUT WITH," SHE SAID. SHE TRIED TO FORCE ANOTHER FLIRTY SMILE ONTO HER LIPS BUT, IT WAS BECOMING MORE AND MORE DIFFICULT FOR HER TO PUT ANY KIND OF EXPRESSION ON HER FACE.

THE ROOM HAD BEGUN TO SPIN QUICKLY AROUND HER AND IT WAS GETTING MORE AND MORE DIFFICULT TO THINK CLEARLY.

"WHAT IF IT WERE TWO OF US?" THE BARMAN ASKED HIS FACE SWIMMING IN FRONT OF HER. SHE HAD JUST OPENED HER MOUTH TO ASK WHAT HE MEANT WHEN SHE FELT A STRONG HAND WITH STRANGE, CLAW-LIKE FINGERS CURL AROUND HER FOREARM.

"IT'LL BE EASIER IF YOU DON'T SCREAM," A

VOICE BEHIND HER SAID. EVEN THROUGH THE HAZE IN HER SPINNING MIND, SHE KNEW THAT SHE HAD NO DESIRE TO OBEY THAT COMMAND.

INSTINCTIVELY, SHE ELBOWED THE MAN IN THE RIBS WITH HER FREE HAND AS THOUGH HE WERE A PATRON AT THE CROWDED BAR. WHEN THIS HAD NO EFFECT, SHE STAMPED ON HIS FOOT CAUSING HIM TO CURSE IN SHOCK AND DROP HER ARM.

AS FAST AS HER MUDDLED MIND WOULD ALLOW SHE PUSHED THE CLUB GOERS ASIDE AND RUSHED TO PETE AT THE END OF THE BAR. HE WAS STILL STARING AT THE DANCE FLOOR WHEN THE MAN WHOSE FACE SHE STILL HADN'T SEEM GRABBED HER ONCE AGAIN FROM BEHIND.

HER HEAD WAS BECOMING HEAVIER BY THE SECOND. SHE FELT AS THOUGH SHE COULD HARDLY KEEP HER EYES OPEN. STILL, SHE KEPT HER EYES ON HER COUSIN AND OPENED HER MOUTH TRYING AS BEST SHE COULD TO SUMMON THE VOICE TO CALL OUT HIS NAME.

"TAKE HER OUTSIDE," THE VOICE OF THE BARMAN SAID. SHE WAS AWARE THAT HE HAD MOVED OUT FROM BEHIND THE BAR NOW HE WAS CASUALLY STANDING BEHIND HER AS THE MAN WITH THE CLAW-LIKE GRIP MANEUVERED HER AWAY FROM PETER.

AS SOON AS THEY TURNED TO MAKE THEIR WAY TO THE DOOR, SHE FELT HER BODY BEGIN TO GROW LIMP. THROUGH THE HAZE THAT WAS COVERING HER MIND, IT WAS NOW CLEAR THAT THE CHARMING BARTENDER HAD SLIPPED SOMETHING OTHER THAN ALCOHOL INTO HER DRINK.

HER HEART THUDDED AND SHE BEGAN TO PANIC AS THE UNSEEN MAN BEHIND HER PRODDED HER TOWARDS THE EXIT, FLANKED BY THE BARTENDER AT HER SIDE. SHE LOOKED FRANTICALLY AROUND THE BAR, HOPING TO FIND SOME AVENUE OF ESCAPE.

FINALLY, HER HAZE FILLED GAZE LANDED ON SETH KILLGORE. A SMALL THRILL OF HOPE WASHED OVER HER WHEN HE TURNED HIS HAUGHTY GAZE FROM THE DANCE FLOOR TO HER.

AS SOON AS HE SAW HER WITH THE TWO MEN AT HER SIDE, HIS EYES NARROWED IN CONFUSION AND CONCERN. SHE COULD TELL IMMEDIATELY THAT HE SAW WHAT THE OTHER PATRONS COULD NOT. EVEN SO, SHE FELT SHE NEEDED TO MAKE SURE HE UNDERSTOOD THE DANGER.
THINKING AS QUICKLY AS SHE COULD, SHE MANAGED TO MOVE HER MOUTH AS SHE PASSED SETH BY THE EXIT.

"HELP ME," SHE WHISPERED AS THEY PRESSED AGAINST HIM. IT WAS BARELY AUDIBLE, FOR HALF A MOMENT, SHE WORRIED THAT HE HADN'T HEARD HER AT ALL.

BUT, A MOMENT LATER, HE GAVE HER A SUBTLE NOD AND TURNED TO TAP HIS BROTHER WHO WAS STILL DANCING ON THE ARM. WITH A STYLISH NOD, HE DIRECTED CAIN'S ATTENTION TO ANDI AND THE MEN WITH HER. WITH ANOTHER NOD, AS THOUGH HE UNDERSTOOD SOMETHING, CAIN STEPPED IN FRONT OF THE MEN, BLOCKING THEIR WAY TO THE EXIT.

"HEY, WHAT ARE YOU DOING WITH MY GIRL?" CAIN ASKED LOUDLY SO THAT HE COULD BE HEARD ABOVE THE MUSIC. SEVERAL OTHER PATRONS SLOWED THEIR DANCING AND TURNED TO WATCH.

"DIDN'T KNOW SHE WAS YOUR GIRL," THE BARTENDER SAID MOVING TOWARDS CAIN MENACINGLY. THE MAN WITH THE CLAWED HAND STILL KEPT HOLD OF ANDI'S ARM. HER BODY WAS BECOMING HEAVY AND THE ANGRY WORDS SETH WAS EXCHANGING WITH THE BARTENDER WERE BEGINNING TO BLUR TOGETHER.

NOT A MINUTE LATER, SHE SAW CAIN REV HIS LARGE BODY UP AND THROW A SURPRISINGLY HARD PUNCH AT THE

BARTENDER. ALMOST AS SOON AS HE DID, SHE HEARD THE MAN BEHIND HER LET OUT A PAINFUL GRUNT AS THOUGH HE HAD BEEN KICKED FROM BEHIND.

ANDI FELT A STRUGGLE BEHIND HER THAT JOSTLED AND TWISTED HER BODY WHICH WAS GROWING LIMPER BY THE MINUTE. FINALLY, SHE HEARD A LOUD, HIGH-PITCHED CRY FROM BEHIND HER. THE BAR FELL SILENT FOR HALF A MOMENT THEN, SEVERAL SCREAMS ERUPTED. ANDI FELT THE MAN WITH THE CLAW DISAPPEAR FROM BEHIND HER AND SAW SOMETHING LIKE A LARGE BAT FLY TOWARDS THE EXIT.

AS PATRONS PUSHED TO MAKE THEIR WAY OUT OF THE CLUB, ANOTHER HAND TOOK HOLD OF HER ARM. SHE BEGAN TO SQUIRM ONCE MORE BEFORE A FAMILIAR VOICE FILLED HER EAR.

"DON'T WORRY. WE'VE GOT YOU NOW," SETH SAID. SHE TURNED TO LOOK AT HIM. HIS EYES, FOR THE FIRST TIME SINCE SHE HAD MET HIM, DID NOT HOLD A HAUGHTY OR ARROGANT EXPRESSION. THEY LOOKED INTO HER GREEN ONES WITH A SOFT, CONCERNED GAZE.

IT WAS THE LAST THING SHE REMEMBERED CLEARLY BEFORE THE WORLD FADED TO BLACK AROUND HER.

Chapter Two

WHAT COULD HAVE BEEN DAYS, HOURS OR MINUTES LATER, ANDI FELT HER CONSCIOUSNESS RETURNING TO HER. SHE BECAME AWARE THAT A PILLOW SAT BENEATH HER HEAD AND A SOFT COVERLET HAD BEEN PLACED OVER HER BODY.

SHE ALSO HAD A POUNDING HEADACHE AND HER LIMBS FELT AS IF THEY'D BEEN RUN THROUGH SOME KIND OF FLOWER MILL. IF THIS WAS WHAT A BAD HANGOVER FELT LIKE, SHE WAS SORRY THAT THIS HAD TO BE HER FIRST EXPERIENCE.

HEAD THROBBING, SHE DIDN'T DARE OPEN HER EYES, SURE THAT THE LIGHT IN THE ROOM WOULD BLIND HER AND MAKE HER CONDITION EVEN WORSE THAN IT WAS. AS HER MIND STRUGGLED TO RETURN FROM ITS SLEEPY HAZE, SHE REALIZED THAT A STRONG, WARM HAND WAS HOLDING TIGHT TO HER LIMP AND CLAMMY ONE.

THE GRIP WAS UNFAMILIAR. WHOEVER IT WAS, SHE WAS SURE IT WAS A MAN. AND, WHAT'S MORE, SHE WAS SURE HE HAD NEVER HELD HER HAND BEFORE.

THAT ALONE ALMOST MADE HER CURIOUS ENOUGH TO BRAVE THE BRIGHT LIGHT THAT SHE COULD TELL FILLED THE ROOM AROUND HER. BEFORE SHE COULD MAKE UP HER MIND, SHE HEARD FOOTSTEPS COME INTO THE ROOM.

"HOW IS SHE?" A VOICE SHE RECOGNIZED AS HER COUSINS ASKED.

"I THINK SHE'S STILL OUT," SETH'S VOICE REPLIED. ANDI FELT AN ODD JOLT IN HER STOMACH WHEN SHE REALIZED IT WAS SETH KILLGORE WHO WAS STILL HOLDING TIGHT TO HER HAND.

THAT NEW INFORMATION CAUSED HER TO ANALYZE THE GRIP THAT HELD HERS FURTHER. HIS HANDS WERE WARMER THAN SHE HAD EXPECTED. AND MUCH STRONGER THAN HIS SLENDER FRAME SUGGESTED.

"YOUR FATHER SAYS HE WANTS TO SEE HER AS SOON AS SHE'S AWAKE," PETE SAID.

HER MIND STOPPED AT THAT AND THEN BEGAN TO WHIRL AGAIN. WHY WOULD SETH'S FATHER WANT TO SPEAK TO HER? SHE'D NEVER MET THE MAN, AFTER ALL.

"IT SHOULDN'T BE LONG NOW," SETH ANSWERED. "I THINK I FELT HER TWITCH."

"WHAT WAS IT THEY GAVE HER?"

20

"I DON'T THINK IT WAS ANYTHING WORSE THAN A SIMPLE DATE RAPE DRUG," HE SAID. "THEY NEED HER ALIVE, AFTER ALL. AT LEAST FOR NOW."

WHO WERE THEY? CLEARLY, SETH WAS TALKING ABOUT THE MEN IN THE CLUB. BUT, THE WAY HE SAID IT MADE IT SOUND AS THOUGH THERE WERE MORE OF THEM OUT THERE SOMEWHERE.
WELL, ANDI REALIZED, THERE WAS ONLY ONE WAY SHE WAS GOING TO FIND OUT WHAT, EXACTLY, WAS HAPPENING. RELUCTANTLY, SHE OPENED HER EYES.

"OH, HOLY FUCK!" SHE IMMEDIATELY EXCLAIMED AS A BRIGHT LIGHT BLAZED IN HER EYES MAKING HER ENTIRE BODY THROB PAINFULLY.

"GOOD MORNING," SETH SAID. WHEN SHE LOOKED UP AT HIM, SHE COULD SEE THAT ANNOYING, SUPERIOR SMIRK ON HIS LIPS ONCE AGAIN. EVEN THROUGH THE POUNDING OF HER HEAD, SHE KNEW SHE WAS ANNOYED WITH HIM.

"MAYBE IT IS FOR YOU," SHE MUTTERED. "WHAT THE HELL HAPPENED LAST NIGHT?"

"YOU WERE DRUGGED," SETH SAID SIMPLY.

"I GATHERED THAT," ANDI SAID WITH A ROLL OF HER EYES. "WHO DID IT?"

SETH LOOKED ABOUT TO RESPOND BUT, PETE GAVE HIM A SIGNIFICANT LOOK.

"WE'LL GET TO THAT LATER," PETE SAID QUICKLY. "HOW DO YOU FEEL?"

"LIKE A STAMPEDE OF ELEPHANTS ARE DANCING ON MY BRAIN," SHE SAID. "WHERE ARE WE?"

"IT'S CALLED WOODHOUSE," SETH SAID. "CAIN AND I GREW UP HERE."

ANDI LOOKED AROUND AT THE SMALL ROOM. EXPOSED, WOODEN LOGS MADE UP THE WALLS AND THROWS AND NORMAN ROCKWELL STYLE PAINTINGS DOTTED THE ROOM MAKING IT LOOK LIKE THE SORT OF BED AND BREAKFAST PLACE ANDI'S GRANDMOTHER MIGHT ENJOY.

"YOU'RE KIDDING," SHE SAID. SHE COULDN'T IMAGINE LARGE, ATHLETIC CAIN OR EVEN COOL AND DISTANT SETH GROWING UP IN A PLACE LIKE THIS.

"I'M NOT," SETH SAID. "MY PARENTS STILL LIVE HERE. YOU'LL MEET THEM AS SOON AS YOU'RE READY."

"LOOK," SHE SAID, PULLING HERSELF PAINFULLY UP ONTO THE PILLOWS."I'M SURE YOUR MOM AND DAD ARE GREAT. BUT, I REALLY DON'T FEEL LIKE MEETING ANYONE RIGHT NOW."

THE TRUTH WAS, SHE FELT LIKE DOING NOTHING BUT PUKING HER LUNGS OUT AND THEN GOING BACK TO SLEEP UNTIL NEXT CHRISTMAS. BUT, WHEN SHE LOOKED AT SETH, HE SHOOK HIS HEAD, THAT ANNOYING SMIRK ON HIS LIPS ONCE MORE.

"YOU DON'T REALLY HAVE A CHOICE," SETH SAID. "DAD INSISTS."

"MIND TELLING ME WHY?"

"WE'LL GET TO THAT LATER," PETER SAID GIVING ANOTHER POINTED LOOK TO SETH WHO HAD,ONCE AGAIN OPENED HIS MOUTH AS THOUGH TO ANSWER ANDI'S INQUIRY. "POI "DEPENDS," SHE SAID. "WILL YOU TELL ME WHAT'S GOING ON IF I SAY 'NO'?"

THEIR AWKWARD SILENCE SPOKE FOR THEM. SETH AND PETE LOOKED AT EACH OTHER AS THOUGH SILENTLY TRYING TO COMMUNICATE THROUGH EYE CONTACT ALONE.

ANDI, MEANWHILE, WAS TRYING HER BEST TO PUSH AWAY THE FOG STILL CLOUDING HER

BRAIN SO THAT SHE COULD THINK. ON THE ONE HAND, SHE REALLY DIDN'T WANT TO DO ANYTHING OTHER THAN SLEEP AT THE MOMENT. ON THE OTHER, SHE WOULD NEVER FIND OUT ANYTHING IF SHE DIDN'T MEET WITH SETH AND CAIN'S PARENTS.

SHE WAS ABOUT TO OPEN HER MOUTH TO GIVE THE TWO SOME KIND OF ANSWER WHEN THE DOOR FLEW OPEN AND CAIN BURST INSIDE.

"DAD SAYS HE CAN'T WAIT," CAIN SAID. "HE THINKS THEY'RE ON THEIR WAY. HE'S GOT TO MEET WITH HER NOW."

SO MUCH FOR MAKING A DECISION.

"CAN YOU GET UP?" SETH ASKED.

"DO I HAVE A CHOICE?"

"NO."

"FINE THEN."

SHE REACHED HER ARMS BEHIND HER AND PUSHED DOWN ON THE MATTRESS, FORCING HERSELF UP FROM THE PILLOWS. THE BLOOD RUSHED TO HER THROBBING HEAD, SQUINTING AGAINST THE LIGHT.

"NEED HELP?" SETH ASKED OFFERING HER

A HAND.

SHE LOOKED AT IT AND THE MEMORY OF SETH'S STRANGELY WARM TOUCH LAST NIGHT CAME FLOODING BACK TO HER. SHE FELT A FLUSH RUSH TO HER FACE AND WAS MORE THAN HALF INCLINED TO ACCEPT HIS OFFER. BUT, WHEN IT CAME DOWN TO IT, HER PRIDE WON OUT.

"I'M FINE, THANKS," SHE SAID BRUSHING HIS HAND AWAY AND STANDING UP ON HER OWN. HER LEGS, SHE DISCOVERED FELT LIKE JELLO ONLY SLIGHTLY LESS STABLE. SHE FELT HERSELF WOBBLING AS CAIN LED THE WAY OUT OF THE ROOM FOLLOWED BY SETH AND PETER. ANDI, NATURALLY, BROUGHT UP THE REAR.

THE HOME, OR..WHEREVER THEY WERE...SUDDENLY LOOKED MUCH LARGER THAN SHE'D BEEN EXPECTING. GIVEN THE CRAMPED AND CUTESY STATE OF THE ROOM SHE'D BEEN LAID OUT IN, SHE WAS EXPECTING A SMALL LOG CABIN FILLED WITH KNICK KNACKS AND CUCKOO CLOCKS.

INSTEAD, THE HALLWAY THEY LED HER THROUGH WAS DARK AND CAVERNOUS WITH HIGH VAULTED CEILINGS. THE ONLY ORNAMENTS ON THE WALLS WERE ORNATE PORTRAITS OF PALE BUT VERY HANDSOME MEN AND WOMEN DRESSED IN PERIOD

CLOTHING.

IT WAS NOT LONG BEFORE THEY REACHED A LARGE FRENCH DOUBLE DOOR WHICH CAIN PUSHED OPEN.

HE STEPPED ASIDE AND HELD THE DOOR OPEN REVEALING A LARGE ROOM WITH TWO LONG TABLES SET IN THE MIDDLE. AT THE HEAD OF BOTH THESE TABLES IN A HIGH-BACKED CHAIR SAT A PALE, SLENDER MAN WHO SAT TALL AND STRAIGHT. HIS DARK, CLIPPED HAIR, SLICKED BACK, REMINDED ANDI SLIGHTLY OF SETH, AS DID THE NOBLE, HAUGHTY LOOK ON HIS FACE.

THIS, CLEARLY, WAS CAIN AND SETH'S FATHER.

BESIDE HIM SAT A WOMAN. THOUGH SHE SAT JUST AS TALL AS THE MAN BESIDE HER, SHE LOOKED MUCH MORE APPROACHABLE. EVEN FROM THE SPOT AT THE DOOR, ANDI COULD SEE THAT THE WOMAN'S LIGHT BROWN HAIR WAS STREAKED WITH GRAY. THE SMALL PINK MOUTH, OUTLINED BY SHARP LAUGH LINES, CURVED UP INTO A SMALL SMILE AS IT REACHED HER WARM, BROWN EYES.

ANDI FOLLOWED SETH AND PETER (IN THAT ORDER) INTO THE ROOM. SHE PASSED CAIN, STILL STANDING AT HIS VANTAGE POINT, HOLDING THE DOOR OPEN FOR THEM, SHE

NOTICED THAT HIS USUALLY CASUAL, SLOPE-BACKED STANCE HAD SUDDENLY BECOME STIFF AND FORMAL. AS THOUGH HE WERE A ROYAL GUARD PRESENTING A PARTY TO THE KING.

THE ROYAL FEELING INCREASED WHEN BOTH SETH AND PETER PROCEEDED TOWARDS THE HEAD OF THE TABLE AND PERFORMED A SLIGHT BOW BEFORE TAKING THEIR SEATS ON EITHER SIDE. ANDI, FEELING VERY AWKWARD MADE HER WAY UP AND GAVE A SLIGHT NOD OF HER HEAD. ABOUT THE MOST, SHE COULD DO IN TERMS OF BOWING UNDER THE CIRCUMSTANCES BEFORE TAKING A SEAT NEXT TO PETER AND ACROSS FROM SETH.

AS SHE SAT, ANDI COULD NOT HELP BUT STARE AT THE BLACK HAIRED MAN WHOSE COLD, GRAY EYES, ENTIRELY DIFFERENT FROM THE HAZEL EYES OF THE WOMAN NEXT TO HIM, STARED RIGHT BACK AT HER. IT WASN'T A GLARE, REALLY. IT WAS A CALCULATED LOOK, AS THOUGH THE MAN WERE SIZING HER UP. FINALLY, WHEN CAIN CLOSED THE DOOR AND SAT DOWN NEXT TO HIS BROTHER, THE MAN OPENED HIS MOUTH.

"SO, YOU WERE ATTACKED?"

EVEN TO ANDI'S HANGOVER-ADDLED BRAIN, IT SOUNDED LIKE AN ACCUSATION.

"THEY HID THEIR SENT IN THE CROWD,"
CAIN ANSWERED. "I DIDN'T SMELL THEM UNTIL
IT WAS TOO LATE."

"EVEN SO," THE MAN SAID. "IT WASN'T A
GOOD IDEA TO SPEND THE EVENING IN A
CROWDED CLUB IN THE FIRST PLACE."

"IT WASN'T OUR IDEA," PETER SAID. THE
GLARE HE SENT ANDI'S WAY FORCED HER TO
FIGHT THROUGH THE SHOCKED SILENCE TO
SPEAK.

"LOOK, IS SOMEONE GOING TO TELL ME
WHAT THE HELL JUST HAPPENED? BECAUSE I
AM WAY TOO TIRED AND STRESSED AND
HUNGOVER TO DEAL WITH ANY MORE
BULLSHIT."

EVERYONE IN THE ROOM TURNED TO LOOK
AT HER WITH VARYING EXPRESSIONS OF
SHOCK. ANDI FOUND THAT SHE TRULY WAS
TOO TIRED AND CONFUSED TO CARE MUCH.
FINALLY, SETH SPOKE.

"LIKE WE SAID," HE TOLD HER, A SUPERIOR
EXPRESSION NOW REPLACING THE ONE OF
SURPRISE. "YOU WERE DRUGGED."

"YEAH, I KNOW THAT GENIUS," ANDI SPAT
BACK AT HIM. "IS ANYONE GOING TO TELL ME
WHO DID IT?"

"THEY'RE CALLED STRIGA," MATTATHIAS' VOICE CALLED OUT, CAUSING ANDI'S HEAD TO SPIN FROM SETH TO THE HEAD OF THE TABLE.

"A ROMANIAN STRAIN OF VAMPIR, PARTICULARLY FANATIC ABOUT THE PURITY OF THE VAMPIR RACE AND VERY VIOLENT."

"THAT WAS THE BLACK THING THAT SCREAMED AND FLEW AWAY JUST BEFORE YOU PASSED OUT," PETER SAID.

"THE CLAW…" ANDI SAID ABSENTLY, SPEAKING ALMOST TO HERSELF. WITHOUT REALIZING IT, SHE LIFTED HER HAND AND TOUCHED HER SHOULDER WHERE THE CLAW LIKE A HAND HAD GRABBED HOLD OF HER FROM BEHIND IN THE CLUB.

"SOMETIMES THEY WORK WITH MURITOR'S," CAIN SAID. ANDI TURNED TO HIM, HER BROW KNIT IN CONFUSION.

"YOU MIGHT CALL THEM FAMILIARS," HE SAID. "HUMANS WHO WORK WITH THE STRIGA. THAT'S PROBABLY WHAT THAT BARMAN YOU MET WAS."

"OK," ANDI SAID QUIETLY. "SO, THIS…STRIGA ATTACKED ME. WHY ME? I MEAN…HOW ARE ALL OF YOU INVOLVED IN THIS?"

"WE'RE INVOLVED," MATTATHIAS SAID.

"BECAUSE WE ARE VAMPIR AS WELL."

ANDI FELT HER HEART SPEED UP IN HER CHEST. HER EYES BLINKED TWICE, VERY SLOWLY, TRYING TO PROCESS WHAT THE MAN AT THE HEAD OF THE TABLE HAD JUST TOLD HER. THEY WEREN'T....THEY COULDN'T BE...SHE MUST HAVE MISHEARD.

"YOU...YOU'RE VAMPIRES?"

"VAMPIR," SETH CORRECTED HER. "I KNOW IT'S A SMALL CHANGE. BUT, GIVEN WESTERN ATTITUDES TOWARDS OUR KIND, WE PREFER THE ORIGINAL PRONUNCIATION."

ANDI TURNED TO HIM, A FAMILIAR IRONIC SMIRK APPEARED ON HIS LIPS. THOUGH NOW, ANDI SAW IT IN A SLIGHTLY MORE SINISTER LIGHT.

SHE TOOK IN HIS VERY PALE SKIN, THE LIGHT EYES, DELICATE STRUCTURE. FOR THE FIRST TIME, SHE TRULY NOTED THE HEAVILY CURTAINED WINDOWS AND THE DIM LIGHT IN THE LARGE ROOM. A MILLION THINGS SHE HAD NEVER THOUGHT TO NOTICE BEFORE NOW CAME INTO FOCUS LIKE SOMEONE HAD PUT THEM UNDER A TELESCOPE.

"SO…" ANDI BEGAN SLOWLY. "YOU'RE VAMPIRES AND PETER IS...WHAT? LIKE...THAT BARTENDER LAST NIGHT...YOUR FAMILIAR?"

"I'M NO FAMILIAR," PETER SAID ALMOST DEFENSIVELY.

"THEN WHAT ARE YOU?" ANDI ASKED FIERCELY. DETERMINED TO GET TO THE BOTTOM OF WHAT WAS GOING ON.

"I'M A PROTECTOR," HE SAID. "ALL THE MEN IN OUR FAMILY ARE."

"WHAT DO YOU MEAN OUR FAMILY?" ANDI ASKED.

"I MEAN, ALL THE FIRSTBORN MEN OF THE COOKE FAMILY ARE SWORN TO PROTECT THE KILLGORE VAMPIR FAMILY WHENEVER POSSIBLE," HE SAID.

"IT'S PART OF A PACT WE MADE WHEN WE FIRST ARRIVED IN THIS COUNTRY," MATTATHIAS SAID. THROUGH A HAZE OF FRUSTRATION, CONFUSION AND ANGER STILL PRESENT, ANDI WAS NOW ABLE TO HEAR A VAGUELY FOREIGN STRAIN IN MATTATHIAS' VOICE. THOUGH HE MAY HAVE BEEN LIVING IN MASSACHUSETTS FOR A LONG TIME, IT WAS CLEAR THAT HE WASN'T BORN IN THE UNITED STATES.

"I SUPPOSE," HE SAID WITH A SMALL SIGH. "WE MAY AS WELL TELL THE ENTIRE STORY. IT BEGINS A LONG TIME AGO. IN AROUND 1620

WHEN I FIRST CAME TO THIS COUNTRY."

"1620?" ANDI SAID INCREDULOUSLY. "ARE YOU SERIOUS?"

MATTATHIAS GAVE HER A SHARP GLARE WHICH PUT PETER'S TO SHAME. IMMEDIATELY, ANDI FELL SILENT.

"MY PARENTS WERE THE LAST OF THE LINE OF THE OLD VAMPIR LEFT. THE STRIGA HAD RECRUITED ALL OF OUR KIND THEY COULD. THOSE WHO THEY COULD NOT CONVERT TO THEIR VIOLENT WAY OF THINKING, THEY KILLED."

"WAIT, WHAT DO YOU MEAN THEIR VIOLENT WAY OF THINKING?" ANDI ASKED. "WHAT EXACTLY MAKES THESE...STRIGA ANY DIFFERENT FROM YOU?"

"TRUE VAMPIR'S ONLY KILL WHEN NECESSARY," SETH SAID. "AND WE USE ALL THE BLOOD IN THE HUMAN BODY. STORE IT UP SO THAT WE DO NOT HAVE TO KILL FOR MONTHS, POSSIBLY YEARS AT A TIME. WE SEEK TO LIVE IN PEACE WITH HUMANS, FOR THE MOST PART."

"THE STRIGA SEE THINGS DIFFERENTLY," MATTATHIAS CONTINUED, THOUGH ANDI THOUGHT SHE SAW HIM GIVE A SLIGHTLY REPROACHFUL LOOK TO HIS SON FOR HIS INTERRUPTION. "THEY BELIEVE THAT WE...THE

VAMPIR...SHOULD TAKE THIS WORLD FOR OURSELVES. ERADICATE HUMANS OR USE THEM SIMPLY AS SOURCES OF FOOD. THEY SEE HUMANS AS OUR NATURAL ENEMY. AND, EACH VAMPIR WHO SEEKS TO LIVE IN HARMONY WITH HUMANITY BECOMES AN ENEMY OF THE STRIGA AS WELL. IT WAS THIS MINDSET THAT CAUSED MY PARENTS DEATH. THE STRIGA SOUGHT THEM OUT AT OUR HOME IN...I SUPPOSE YOU WOULD CALL IT ALBANIA NOW."

EASTERN EUROPEAN THEN, ANDI THOUGHT TO HERSELF. AT LEAST NOW SHE KNEW WHERE THIS MAN WAS FROM.

"THERE WERE MANY OF THEM," HE REMEMBERED. "FAR MORE OF THEM THAN OF US. I WAS YOUNG AT THE TIME. OH YES," HE SAID LOOKING AT THE SURPRISED EXPRESSION ON ANDI'S FACE. "VAMPIRES DO AGE. JUST AT A MUCH SLOWER RATE THAN YOU DO."

ANDI FELT A FRUSTRATED TINGLE RISE UP THROUGH HER AS SHE TURNED TO SEE SETH AND HIS BROTHER, CAIN EXCHANGE AMUSED GLANCES. CLEARLY LAUGHING AT HER EXPENSE. SHE OPENED HER MOUTH TO TELL THEM OFF BUT, AS SOON AS SHE DID, MATTATHIAS CONTINUED.

"AS SOON AS THEY SURROUNDED THE HOME, MY FATHER TOLD ME TO SLIP OUT THROUGH THE BACK OF OUR HOME AND RUN

AS FAST AND AS FAR AS I COULD. I DID.
EVENTUALLY, I FOUND MYSELF IN ENGLAND.
PLYMOUTH, TO BE EXACT. I HIRED MYSELF OUT
AS A SAILOR. I DIDN'T KNOW MUCH ABOUT THE
SEA BUT, I WAS A QUICK STUDY AND SO
CONFIDENT THAT EVEN THE OLDER SAILORS
ACCEPTED ME. I WAS ABLE TO HIDE MY
NATURE FOR SEVERAL WEEKS BEFORE I WAS
FOUND OUT."

HE PAUSED HERE, HIS PALE THROAT GIVING
A HARD SWALLOW AS THOUGH THE MEMORY
OF THE TALE HE WAS ABOUT TO TELL STAYED
VERY CLEARLY WITH HIM.

"WE HAD BEEN SAILING FOR SIX WEEKS. I'D
NEARLY RUN OUT OF THE BOTTLES OF FRESH
BLOOD I'D STORED AWAY IN A SECRET SPOT
ON THE SHIP. I BEGAN TO GROW HUNGRY AND
MORE THAN A BIT WEAK. EVEN SO, MY SENSES
WERE SHARPER THAN THAT OF MY SHIPMATES.
THAT WAS WHY I HEARD A WOMAN'S SMALL,
SOFT CRY ON ONE OF THE LOWER DECKS
BEFORE ANYONE ELSE COULD. I RUSHED
TOWARDS IT AND FOUND A YOUNG GIRL. NO
MORE THAN THIRTEEN OR FOURTEEN YEARS
OLD, PINNED BENEATH A MAN TWO OR THREE
TIMES HER SIZE."

ANDI, REMEMBERING THE FEELING OF
HELPLESSNESS AS THE LARGE HANDS CLOSED
IN ON HER AT THE CLUB THE NIGHT BEFORE,
HAD NO TROUBLE IMAGINING WHAT A SCENE

LIKE THAT MUST HAVE FELT LIKE TO A YOUNG
WOMAN. THE THOUGHT MADE HER SHIVER
AND, INSTINCTIVELY, SHE CROSSED HER ARMS
AND RUBBED AT THEM FIERCELY.

"I FLEW AT THE MAN. I KNEW HIM TO BE
ONE OF THE YOUNG SAILORS WITH ME, I
SMELLED THE STENCH OF ALCOHOL ON HIS
BREATH. NONE OF THAT STOPPED ME. I
SUPPOSE I WAS SO HUNGRY FROM TOO LITTLE
BLOOD, NOT TO MENTION ANGRY AT THE LOSS
OF MY PARENTS, ANGRY WITH MYSELF FOR
NOT BEING ABLE TO DO ANYTHING THAT, IN
THAT MOMENT, I COULDN'T STOP TO THINK. I
BIT DOWN HARD AT THE MAN'S THROAT AND
SUCKED ALL THE BLOOD I COULD FROM HIM.
THE NEXT THING I KNEW, THE GIRL I'D
RESCUED WAS STANDING AT THE DOOR OF
THE ROOM ALONG WITH ANOTHER MAN WHO
SHE WAS HIDDEN BEHIND. THEY WERE BOTH
STARING AT ME AS THOUGH I WERE THE DEVIL
HIMSELF AND I SUPPOSE TO THEM I WAS."

MATTATHIAS ALLOWED HIMSELF A SMALL
SMILE AT THAT.

"THE MAN'S NAME, AS IT HAPPENED, WAS
FRANCIS COOKE. I TOLD HIM WHAT HAPPENED
AND THE GIRL, MARY CHILTON, CONFIRMED
MY STORY. EVEN SO, I WAS CERTAIN MR. COOKE
WAS GOING TO HAVE ME THROWN OFF THE
SHIP OR REPORTED. INSTEAD, TO MY SURPRISE
AND RELIEF, HE HELPED ME DISPOSE OF THE

35

DRUNKEN SAILORS BODY QUIETLY. IN RETURN, I PLEDGED TO REPAY HIM IN WHATEVER WAY I COULD. THAT WAS HOW THE CONTRACT CAME TO BE SIGNED."

"WHAT CONTRACT?" ANDI ASKED LOOKING AROUND THE TABLE.

"WHEN THE MAYFLOWER CONTRACT WAS SIGNED BETWEEN THE MEN ON THAT FIRST JOURNEY," MATTATHIAS CONTINUED, IN ANSWER TO HER QUESTION. "ANOTHER WAS SIGNED IN SECRET BETWEEN MATTATHIAS KILLGORE AND FRANCIS COOKE. IT STATED THAT, IF MR. COOKE AND ANY IN HIS FAMILY WOULD KEEP MY SECRET, I AND ANY FAMILY I MIGHT HAVE, WOULD VOW TO HARM NO INNOCENT MEN OR WOMEN UPON THIS CONTINENT. I VOWED THAT WE, THE VAMPIR'S WOULD ACT INSTEAD AS ANGELS OF JUSTICE. FEEDING ONLY UPON SOULS WHO PERFORMED THE FOULEST DEEDS AND DEFENDING THEIR INNOCENT VICTIMS. IN RETURN, COOKE PROMISED THAT HE AND HIS SON, AND ANY SON'S HIS SON MIGHT HAVE, WOULD PROTECT ME AND MY KIND FROM ANY WHO WOULD DO US HARM. THE CONTRACT REMAINS IN EFFECT TO THIS DAY."

"THAT'S ALL WELL AND GOOD," ANDI SAID. "BUT, I STILL DON'T SEE WHAT THAT HAS TO DO WITH ME."

"THERE WAS ANOTHER PROVISION IN THE CONTRACT," MATTATHIAS SAID. "WE AGREED THAT, IN ORDER TO SEAL THIS PACT, COOKE WOULD GIVE ME HIS FIRST BORN DAUGHTER AS A MATE. OF COURSE, HE PREFERRED THE TERM WIFE. THOUGH I TOLD HIM, THEY ARE, IN ESSENCE, THE SAME THING. THAT IS HOW I RECEIVED MY LOVELY WIFE, CLARA."

AT THIS POINT, THE WOMAN SEATED NEXT TO MATTHIAS WAS ACKNOWLEDGED FOR THE FIRST TIME. SHE GAVE ANDI A WARM AND, SOMEWHAT UNDERSTANDING SMILE BUT REMAINED SILENT AS SHE HAD BEEN THROUGHOUT.

"THE ACT OF COOKE DAUGHTERS BEING MATED TO VAMPIR'S WAS TO CONTINUE DOWN THE GENERATIONS," MATTATHIAS SAID. "ONLY WHEN THE LINE STOPPED WOULD THE CONTRACT BE BROKEN."

ANDI LOOKED AT THEM ALL, STRUGGLING TO UNDERSTAND WHAT SHE HAD JUST BEEN TOLD.

"SO, YOU'RE SAYING THAT FOR THIS...THIS...CONTRACT TO REMAIN IN EFFECT..."

"A COOKE DAUGHTER MUST BE MATED TO MY SUCCESSOR," MATTATHIAS SAID. "IN THIS CASE, THE COOKE DAUGHTER IS YOU. AND MY

SUCCESSOR IS-"

"ME," SETH FINISHED FOR HIM. ANDI TURNED QUICKLY FROM MATTATHIAS TO SETH, ACROSS THE TABLE FROM HER. FOR THE FIRST TIME SINCE SHE'D MET HIM, HIS PALE CHEEKS FLUSHED SLIGHTLY PINK WITH EMBARRASSMENT AND HE GLANCED DOWN AT THE FLOOR, REFUSING TO MEET HER EYES. ANDI COULDN'T BLAME HIM.

"YOU MEAN...YOU EXPECT ME TO...GET MARRIED?" ANDI ASKED. HER WORDS WERE SLOW BUT HER THOUGHTS WERE A QUICKLY SPINNING MESS. SHE TURNED TO LOOK AT PETER, PRAYING THAT HE WOULD LAUGH AND TELL HER IT WAS ALL SOME ELABORATE PRANK.

BUT THERE WAS NO LAUGHTER IN HIS EYES WHEN SHE LOOKED AT HIM. HE LOOKED AS EMBARRASSED AS SETH, HIS EYES GLANCING DOWN APOLOGETIC BUT ENTIRELY SERIOUS.

"ANDI, IF WE WANT TO KEEP THE CONTRACT," HE SAID. "THEN...YEAH. YOU'VE GOT TO GET MARRIED."

"MATED," CAIN CORRECTED. ANDI, HER HEAD FEELING AS THOUGH IT WERE ON A SWIVEL, TURNED NOW TO HIM. SHE WAS SURPRISED TO SEE THAT THERE WAS NO EMPATHY IN CAIN'S FACE. INSTEAD, HE

38

GLANCED FROM HIS BROTHER TO ANDI LOOKING SLIGHTLY SULLEN. "IT'S A LITTLE DIFFERENT THAN MARRIAGE."

"NOT MUCH," SETH SAID. HIS TONE WAS SHARP AS THOUGH HE WAS WARNING HIS BROTHER NOT TO SAY TOO MUCH. CAIN GLARED AT HIM FOR A MOMENT BUT THEN, MERELY SHRUGGED AND TURNED TO STARE AHEAD.

"BUT, WHAT IF I DON'T WANT TO GET MARRIED?" ANDI ASKED.

"YOU CAN, OF COURSE, REFUSE," MATTATHIAS SAID. "BUT, IF YOU DO, THE CONTRACT BECOMES NULL."

"WHAT HAPPENS THEN?"

"WELL, SEEING AS WE ARE THE ONLY CLAN OF OLD VAMPIR LEFT IN THE NEW WORLD AND THERE ARE NO MORE THAN ONE HUNDRED OF US," SETH BEGAN. "WE RELY ON THE MEN OF YOUR FAMILY TO HELP US."

"NOT TO MENTION," CLARA SAID "THE MATING BETWEEN HUMANS AND VAMPIRES HAS KEPT THE BALANCE BETWEEN THE TWO PEOPLE FOR CENTURIES. IF THE MATING DOESN'T OCCUR…"

"THE SCALES WILL FALL TO EITHER ONE

SIDE OR THE OTHER," SETH SAID. "AND, SINCE THE STRIGA ARE SO MUCH STRONGER...IT DOESN'T LOOK GOOD FOR HUMANITY."

ANDI SAT BACK IN HER CHAIR, HEAD REELING. SEARCHING THROUGH EVERYTHING SHE HAD JUST BEEN TOLD, ALL THE MOUNDS OF INFORMATION SHE HAD JUST BEEN GIVEN, SHE TRIED TO FIND SOME KIND OF CHOICE IN WHAT SHE HAD BEEN TOLD. A WAY THAT SHE COULD PREVENT THIS...BALANCE...OR WHATEVER IT WAS FROM BEING DISTORTED BUT STILL WOULDN'T HAVE TO MARRY SETH.

"BUT, WAIT," SHE SAID. "IF THESE STRIGA ARE SO POWERFUL, HOW HAVE YOU AND A HANDFUL OF HUMANS BEEN ABLE TO HOLD THEM OFF THIS LONG ANYWAY?"

"BECAUSE OF ME," CAIN SAID SUDDENLY. ANDI'S HEAD SWIVELED TO HIM. WHEN IT DID, SHE FOUND MORE THAN A HINT OF PRIDE IN BOTH HIS VOICE AND EXPRESSION.

"BECAUSE OF CREATURES LIKE YOU," SETH SAID. NOW, ANDI OBSERVED, IT WAS HIS TURN TO SOUND SLIGHTLY SULLEN.

"CAIN IS WHAT THEY CALL A DYMPHIRE. HALF HUMAN AND HALF VAMPIRE. THE CLAN IS MADE UP OF THEM. CHILDREN OF UNIONS BETWEEN COOKE WOMAN AND VAMPIR MEN."

"WE'RE AS STRONG AS THE STRIGA," CAIN SAID. "BUT WITH NONE OF THE WEAKNESSES. WE DON'T NEED HUMAN BLOOD. AND WE CAN ATTACK THEM IN THE DAYLIGHT."

"AND THAT IS WHY A MATING BETWEEN A HUMAN WOMAN AND MATTATHIAS' SUCCESSOR IS SO ESSENTIAL," THE WOMAN SAID. "WITHOUT THE DYMPHIRE, THE STRIGA WILL OVERTAKE US AND THE HUMANS WE PROTECT WITHIN A MATTER OF YEARS. WE NEED A NEW DYMPHIRE GENERATION TO CARRY ON THE LINE."

"THAT IS ALSO WHY WE NEED YOUR DECISION," MATTATHIAS SAID. THOUGH HIS VOICE WAS STILL CALM, IT CARRIED A HINT OF IMPATIENCE. WHEN ANDI LOOKED ABOUT THE ROOM, SHE COULD SEE EACH OF THE MEMBERS OF THEIR LITTLE CONGREGATION STARING AT HER.

UNABLE TO THINK OF ANYTHING THAT MIGHT STALL THE PROCESS FURTHER, BUT UNABLE TO GIVE AN ANSWER, SHE BROUGHT ONE HAND TO HER MOUTH AND BEGAN TO BITE AT HER NAIL. THIS WAS A HABIT SHE'D HAD SINCE SHE WAS YOUNG AND SHE ALWAYS FELL BACK ON IT WHEN SHE WAS STRESSED.

SHE TURNED HER EYES TO SETH. THOUGH HIS PALE FACE WAS STILL SLIGHTLY FLUSHED, HIS GRAY EYES HAD, AT LAST MET HERS. SHE

41

WAS GLAD TO SEE THE SAME RELUCTANCE AND UNCERTAINTY THAT SHE FELT WRITTEN IN HIS FACE AS WELL. IT WAS A CHANGE, ANYWAY, FROM THE COCKY SMIRK HE USUALLY CARRIED.

"SO, IF I SAY NO," SHE SAID SLOWLY. "BASICALLY, THESE OTHER VAMPIRES...THESE...STRIGA...WILL GO CRAZY AND TAKE OVER THE WORLD AS WE KNOW IT?"

"BASICALLY," PETER SAID. EVEN THOUGH HER COUSIN SPOKE, SHE DIDN'T TURN TO HIM. SHE KEPT HER EYES, INSTEAD, ON SETH. SHE LOOKED HER, APPARENTLY, INTENDED HUSBAND UP AND DOWN. HIS SLIGHTLY LONG DARK HAIR FELL INTO HIS GRAY EYES AND SHE FOLLOWED HIS LONG NECK FALLING TOWARDS THE OPENING OF HIS BLACK SHIRT THAT REVEALED A SHARP, PALE COLLARBONE.

SHE HAD TO ADMIT, HE WAS GOOD LOOKING. AND, DESPITE HIS SLENDER BUILD, SHE COULD SEE THAT HE WAS BUILT MORE STRONGLY THAN HE LOOKED AT FIRST GLANCE.

WHEN HER GAZE MOVED BACK UP TO HIS FACE, HOWEVER, THE SUPERIOR SMIRK WAS BACK. CLEARLY, HE'D BEEN TAKING STOCK OF HER AS WELL, AND HE HADN'T BEEN NEARLY AS IMPRESSED.

THAT LOOK ALMOST MADE HER SAY NO
AND SCREW HUMANITY. BUT, WHEN SHE
LOOKED BACK TO MATTATHIAS, SHE CAUGHT
HER COUSIN'S GAZE.

SHE AND PETER HAD ALWAYS BEEN CLOSE.
THEY'D SPENT EVERY SUMMER TOGETHER
SINCE THEY WERE TWO. AND, WHEN HE
LOOKED AT ANDI, HIS BROWN EYES WIDE, SHE
KNEW HE WAS PLEADING WITH HER. AND, AS
USUAL, SHE COULDN'T LET HIM DOWN.

"WELL, I GUESS I DON'T HAVE A CHOICE,"
ANDI SAID FINALLY. "SO, YEAH. I'LL DO IT."

MATTATHIAS GAVE THE FIRST SMILE ANDI
HAD YET SEEN FROM HIM. IT LOOKED EVERY
BIT AS PUFFED UP AND ARROGANT AS HIS SONS.

"I THOUGHT YOU WOULD," HE SAID. "NOW,
THE MATING CEREMONY WILL BEGIN IN ONE
MONTH. YOU WILL REMAIN HERE UNTIL
TOMORROW EVENING. THEN, SETH, CAIN, AND
PETER WILL TAKE YOU TO THE SAFE HOUSE IN
BOSTON. YOU'LL GO TO NEW YORK FROM
THERE."

"NEW YORK?" ANDI ASKED.

"THAT'S WHERE THE CEREMONY TAKES
PLACE," SETH SAID. "IT'S KIND OF OUR CLAN'S
HEADQUARTERS."

"NOW," MATTATHIAS SAID STANDING FROM THE HEAD OF THE TABLE. "CLARA WILL SHOW YOU TO YOUR ROOM. YOU SHOULD REST. YOU'LL NEED IT."

THE WOMAN AT MATTATHIAS' SIDE STOOD AND MOVED TO ANDI'S SIDE. SHE TOOK HER GENTLY BY THE ARM AND GAVE HER ANOTHER SMILE THAT, ANDI HOPED WAS LACED WITH UNDERSTANDING. EITHER WAY, IT ENCOURAGED ANDI TO FOLLOW

SHE FOLLOWED CLARA DOWN THE DARK CORRIDOR, THIS TIME TAKING STOCK OF THE CURTAINS OVER THE WINDOWS. CLARA CARRIED A SMALL LANTERN IN FRONT OF THEM THAT LOOKED ANTIQUE, THOUGH, ANDI COULD TELL THAT IT WAS OUTFITTED WITH AN ELECTRIC LIGHT BULB.

"SO…" ANDI BEGAN AWKWARDLY AS THEY PASSED DARKLY PAINTED DOORS ON EITHER SIDE OF THE HALLWAY. "YOU'RE NOT A VAMPIRE, BUT EVERYONE ELSE IS?"

"MOST OF THE OTHERS ARE," CLARA SAID. "A FEW ARE DYMPHIR. HALF VAMPIRES LIKE CAIN. A FEW OF THE WOMEN ARE LIKE YOU AND ME."

"YOU MEAN…MATES FOR THE MEN?" ANDI ASKED.

"YES," CLARA SAID. "YOU'RE RELATED TO ALL OF THEM. IF ONLY DISTANTLY. HERE WE ARE."

THEY STOPPED IN FRONT OF THE LARGEST SET OF DOORS ANDI HAD YET SEEN IN THE HALLWAY.

"THEY CALL THIS THE MATE'S ROOM," CLARA SAID OPENING THE DOOR. "IT'S THE SECOND LARGEST IN THE HOME. THE LARGEST, OF COURSE, IS MATTATHIAS AND MINE."

CLARA FLIPPED ON THE LIGHT SWITCH TO REVEAL THE LARGEST ROOM ANDI HAD EVER SEEN. TRUTHFULLY IT WAS MORE OF AN APARTMENT. THERE WAS A LARGE WINDOW, THIS ONE UNCOVERED AND THE BRIGHT SUNLIGHT, TOO BRIGHT FOR ANDI'S STILL HUNGOVER TASTES, SPILLED THROUGH IT ONTO A VELVET WINDOW SEAT BENEATH. THIS WAS FLANKED BY TWO BOOKCASES FILLED TO THE BRIM WITH LARGE BOOKS, SOME OF WHICH LOOKED ANTIQUE.

ON THE OTHER SIDE OF THE ROOM WAS A LARGE BED, SURELY KINGSIZE, WITH A SHEER CANOPY OVER TOP. THERE WAS ALSO A VANITY WITH DOZENS OF MAKEUP CHOICES AND PERFUME BOTTLES.

"THERE IS A BATHROOM AROUND THE CORNER," CLARA TOLD HER. "IT SHOULD BE

OUTFITTED WITH EVERYTHING YOU NEED."

"I...THANKS," ANDI SAID STILL FEELING FLUSTERED AND MORE THAN A BIT DISORIENTED.

"I UNDERSTAND, YOU KNOW," CLARA SAID SUDDENLY. ANDI TURNED FROM HER AWED INSPECTION OF THE BED TO FACE CLARA. HER EYES NARROWED INCREDULOUSLY. CLARA GAVE ANOTHER UNDERSTANDING SMILE.

"I REMEMBER FEELING CONFUSED AND...FRIGHTENED...WHEN MY FATHER TOLD ME WHAT I HAD TO DO," SHE SAID. "THAT I HAD TO BE...MATTED TO MATTATHIAS. BUT IN TIME, I CAME TO LOVE HIM VERY MUCH."

"THAT'S GREAT FOR YOU," ANDI SAID "BUT, AT THE MOMENT, I DON'T THINK I CAN THINK ABOUT ANYTHING PAST TOMORROW. LET ALONE WHETHER OR NOT I'LL EVENTUALLY LOVE MY...HUSBAND...OR WHATEVER HE'LL BE."

"I KNOW IT SEEMS HOPELESS," CLARA SAID. "BUT, SETH IS A GOOD MAN. GIVE IT TIME AND YOU'LL SEE."

"YEAH, OK," ANDI SAID RELUCTANTLY. SHE TRIED TO FORCE A SMILE BUT SHE WASN'T SURE THAT SHE MANAGED IT. EITHER WAY, CLARA DIDN'T SEEM IN THE MOOD TO PRESS IT FURTHER.

"I'LL LET YOU GET SOME REST," SHE SAID. "GOOD NIGHT."

ANDI, FINDING HERSELF BEYOND TIRED, DISCOVERED THAT SHE COULD DO NOTHING MORE THAN NOD.

SHE WATCHED AS CLARA CLOSED THE HUGE DOUBLE DOORS LEAVING ANDI ALONE IN THE UNFAMILIAR ROOM. AS SHE SLID INTO THE BED AND LAID HER STILL THROBBING HEAD DOWN ON THE PILLOW, HER MIND STILL REELING, SHE HAD NO IDEA HOW GOOD HER SLEEP WAS GOING TO BE.

Chapter Three

IT TURNED OUT THAT ANDI'S SLEEP WAS NOT NEARLY AS GOOD AS ANYONE HAD HOPED. HER MIND KEPT GIVING HER VISIONS OF GIANT, PALE FLYING BLACK CREATURES INTERMIXED WITH FLOWING BLOOD. SETH DANCED IN AND OUT OF HER NIGHTMARES. SOMETIMES AS A WELCOME REPRIEVE, SOMETIMES AS AN OMINOUS PRESENCE, HIDING AT THE EDGE OF HER CONSCIOUSNESS, READY TO STRIKE OUT AT ANY MOMENT.

IT WAS HIS VOICE, SAYING SOMETHING INCOMPREHENSIBLE, THAT PLAYED IN HER HEAD WHEN SHE WAS JOLTED AWAKE FOR WHAT FELT LIKE THE SEVENTH TIME THAT DAY. WHEN HER EYES OPENED, STILL FUZZY WITH SLEEP, SHE REALIZED THAT THE SOUND OF HIS VOICE WAS STILL BUZZING IN HER EAR.

AS THE LAGGING FEELING OF SLEEP BEGAN TO FADE, SHE RECOGNIZED THAT IT WASN'T SIMPLY A HALF-REMEMBERED PORTION OF THE DREAM. HIS VOICE, TRULY, WAS SOUNDING FROM THE HALLWAY JUST OUTSIDE HER DOOR. ACCOMPANIED BY THE VOICE OF A WOMAN. CLARA.

ANDI SAT UP IN HER LUXURIOUS BED AND

GLANCED OUT THE WINDOW. THE SUN, THOUGH HANGING LOW IN THE SKY, STILL HAD NOT SET. SEEING AS SHE WAS, NOW, SURROUNDED BY VAMPIRES, SHE WAS SURPRISED THAT SHE WAS NOT THE ONLY ONE IN THE HOUSE AWAKE.

SETH'S VOICE GREW LOUDER AS SHE PADDED, SOFTLY, TOWARDS THE DOOR. THE BETTER TO HEAR HIS CONVERSATION.

"...MOM, I WON'T FORCE HER TO MATE WITH ME. I CAN'T!"

"IT'S NOT FORCE," CLARA WAS SAYING GENTLY. "THE GIRL HAD A CHOICE JUST AS I DID."

"SOME CHOICE," HE SAID WITH AN IRONIC SNORT. "EITHER BED SOME GUY YOU DON'T KNOW OR BE RESPONSIBLE FOR THE DESTRUCTION OF THE HUMAN RACE."

"WELL, WHEN YOU PUT IT THAT WAY, IT SOUNDS RATHER DRAMATIC."

"IT IS!" SETH SAID URGENTLY. "WHAT DECENT PERSON WOULD GAMBLE WITH THE FATE OF THE WORLD?"

"YOU WOULD BE SURPRISED WHAT PEOPLE WOULD DO WHEN THEIR HAPPINESS IS AT STAKE," CLARA SAID. "I MADE MY DECISION

THE SAME AS ANDI DID AND I HAVEN'T
REGRETTED IT SINCE. SHE WON'T EITHER. I
PROMISE YOU."

"WHAT IF SHE DOES?" SETH ASKED. "WHAT
IF…"

"WOULD YOU HAVE CHOSEN HER IF YOU
THOUGHT SHE WOULDN'T BE HAPPY WITH
YOU?"

CHOSEN? ANDI'S BROW FURROWED AT THE
WORD. NO ONE SAID ANYTHING ABOUT SETH
HAVING A CHOICE IN THE MATTER. FROM
WHAT ANDI HAD GLEANED FROM THE BRIEF
MEETING WITH MATTATHIAS, SHE'D ASSUMED
THAT SETH WAS BEING, ESSENTIALLY, FORCED
INTO THIS JUST AS SHE WAS.

"CHOICE," HE MUTTERED. "IT WASN'T MUCH
OF A CHOICE FOR ME EITHER. JUST A…A
FEELING."

"AND DID YOU GET THIS…FEELING…WITH
ANY OF THE OTHER COUSINS PETER BROUGHT
TO MEET YOU?"

THERE WAS A PAUSE AND ANDI TRIED TO
IMAGINE SETH GIVING SOME SILENT ANSWER
TO HIS MOTHER.

"YOU SEE?" CLARA ASKED IN A REASSURING
VOICE. "YOUR INSTINCTS CHOSE ANDI FOR

YOU. THE INSTINCTS YOU HAVE ARE GOOD. YOU SHOULD TRUST THEM."

"BUT, HOW CAN I TRUST THEM?" HE ASKED. THERE WAS A SHAKING DESPERATION TO HIS VOICE WHICH ANDI DIDN'T FULLY UNDERSTAND. "HOW CAN I TRUST THEM WHEN EVERY TIME I LOOK AT HER SOMETHING INSIDE ME WANTS TO...TO…"

HE LET HIS VOICE TRAIL AWAY AND DIE AS THOUGH THE THOUGHT OF WHAT HE WANTED WAS TOO HORRIBLE TO VOICE. ANDI HEARD CLARA HEAVE A SIGH.

"SETH," SHE SAID, GENTLY. "I DON'T PRETEND TO KNOW WHAT IT IS TO...FEEL...WHAT YOU FEEL. TO HAVE THE THIRST THAT YOU HAVE. I DO KNOW THAT YOUR FATHER FELT THAT WAY ABOUT ME. AS FAR AS I KNOW, HE STILL DOES. HE FOUGHT AGAINST IT. THAT FIGHT WITHIN HIM IS WHAT MAKES HIM LOVE ME MORE. IT MAKES ME LOVE HIM. IT WILL BE THE SAME FOR YOU."

"YOU CAN'T KNOW THAT," HE SAID.

"I DO."

THERE WAS A LONGER PAUSE HERE. NOW, TRY AS ANDI MIGHT, SHE COULDN'T BEGIN TO IMAGINE THE LOOK THAT MIGHT HAVE PASSED BETWEEN THE MOTHER AND SON.

"IT SHOULDN'T HAVE BEEN ME," HE SAID FINALLY. "THE SUCCESSOR IS SUPPOSED TO BE A DYMPHIRE. A HALF BREED BETWEEN A HUMAN AND A VAMPIRE. CAIN IS YOUR SON. HE SHOULD-"

"YOU ARE OUR SON JUST AS MUCH AS YOUR BROTHER," CLARA SAID INSISTENTLY.

"BUT I'M NOT-"

"IT'S NOT ABOUT WHAT YOU ARE OR ARE NOT," SETH'S MOTHER TOLD HIM. "IT IS ABOUT WHO YOU ARE. YOUR BROTHER DOES NOT HAVE THE STRENGTH OF CHARACTER YOU POSSESS. I KNEW, EVEN WHEN HE WAS A CHILD, HE COULD NEVER TAKE ON SUCH A RESPONSIBILITY. THAT IS WHY I CHOSE FOR YOU TO REMAIN YOUR FATHER'S SUCCESSOR. IT IS THE MATE'S CHOICE- MY CHOICE- TO MAKE. JUST AS IT WILL BE ANDI'S ONE DAY."
"WHAT IF SHE DOESN'T-?"

"DO YOU WANT THIS GIRL?" CLARA ASKED CUTTING HIM OFF WITH A NOTE OF IMPATIENCE.

"YES," SETH ANSWERED QUIETLY. ANDI'S HEART BEGAN TO BEAT WILDLY INSIDE HER CHEST. "I DON'T KNOW QUITE WHY. BUT...I DO...I DO WANT HER. I HAVE EVER SINCE I SAW HER."

53

"WELL THEN," CLARA SAID WITH AN AIR OF FINALITY. "YOU HAVE AT LEAST ONE MONTH TO PROVE TO YOURSELF THAT YOU DESERVE HER."

ANDI HEARD A PAIR OF FOOTSTEPS MOVING CLOSER TO THE DOOR.

"THE SUN'S NEARLY SET," CLARA SAID. "YOU'D BEST GO GET READY. AND...I THINK...MAYBE YOU SHOULD WAKE ANDI WHEN YOU'RE READY TO GO."

"MOM, I-"

"SHE HAS A RIGHT TO GET TO KNOW THE MAN SHE'S ABOUT TO MARRY," CLARA SAID FIRMLY. "NOW, OFF TO YOUR ROOM. FINISH PACKING."

ANDI LISTENED TO THEIR FOOTSTEPS UNTIL THEY FADED DOWN THE HALLWAY. SHE MOVED BACK TO HER BED BUT DIDN'T LIE DOWN IN IT. SHE HAD ABSOLUTELY NO DESIRE TO SLEEP. ABOUT A SECOND AFTER SITTING IN THE BED, SHE MOVED INSTEAD TO THE WINDOW SEAT.

THE VIEW OUTSIDE WAS ONE OF TALL PINE TREES SHADING A VIEW OF THE SETTING SUN. SHE STARED OUT THE LARGE WINDOW INTO THIS PEACEFUL WOODED LANDSCAPE TRYING

TO PROCESS WHAT SHE HAD JUST HEARD.

SETH...CHOSE...HER AS HIS MATE.
SETH...WANTED HER. SHE HONESTLY WASN'T
SURE HOW THAT WAS POSSIBLE. THEY'D MET
NOT MORE THAN TWO DAYS BEFORE. THOUGH,
SHE SUPPOSED, HE HAD SAID HE WANTED HER,
IMPLYING LUST, NOT LOVE. LORD KNOWS
SHE'D LUSTED AFTER MEN WHO SHE'D ONLY
KNOWN A FEW MINUTES.

BUT, SHE WOULDN'T CONTEMPLATE
MARRYING SAID, MEN. NOT EVEN SLEEPING
WITH THEM. AT LEAST NOT UNTIL THEY'D
TAKEN HER ON AT LEAST THREE LEGITIMATE
DATES.

NOW, SHE WAS EXPECTED TO MARRY A
VIRTUAL STRANGER. A STRANGER WHO
WANTED HER, SURE. AND, SHE HAD TO ADMIT,
A GOOD LOOKING STRANGER. BUT, A
STRANGER NONE THE LESS.

ADD TO THAT FACT THAT HE WAS A
VAMPIRE AND SHE THOUGHT HER SITUATION
JUST MIGHT BE ONE OF THE MOST UNIQUE IN
THE HISTORY OF HUMAN MATING.

AND, SHE WASN'T EVEN GOING TO BEGIN
TO GET INTO THAT WHOLE THING ABOUT CAIN
BEING THE ONE WHO WAS, APPARENTLY,
SUPPOSED TO HAVE MATED WITH HER. SHE
WASN'T QUITE SURE HOW THAT WOULD'VE

CHANGED THINGS. AND SHE WASN'T SURE WHICH MAN IF EITHER, SHE WOULD HAVE PREFERRED.

ALL OF THIS PLAYED OVER AND OVER AGAIN INSIDE HER MIND AS SHE WATCHED THE WIND BLOW THROUGH THE TREES, THE ORANGE AND PINK OF THE SETTING SUN CASTING LONG SHADOWS ON THE GROUND OUTSIDE HER WINDOW.

SHE JUMPED ABOUT A FOOT IN THE AIR WHEN A LOUD KNOCK CAME FROM HER DOOR.

"COME IN," SHE CALLED.

ANDI DIDN'T NEED TO TURN AND LOOK IN ORDER TO SEE WHO IT WAS WHEN THE DOOR CREAKED OPEN. EVEN SO, SHE TURNED AND FACED SETH, HER MIND SPINNING WITH QUESTIONS SHE WASN'T SURE SHE COULD BRING HERSELF TO ASK.

"I THOUGHT I SHOULD GET YOU UP," HE SAID AWKWARDLY. "WE'RE GETTING READY TO GO."

"GO WHERE, EXACTLY?" ANDI ASKED.

"THERE'S A SAFE HOUSE A LITTLE OUTSIDE OF BOSTON," HE SAID. "WE'LL GO THERE FIRST."

"AND THEN ON TO NEW YORK?"

"THAT'S THE IDEA."

ANOTHER SMIRK CROSSED OVER HIS FACE. THE ONE THAT ALWAYS MADE HER FEEL LIKE HE WAS LAUGHING AT HER. SHE FROWNED AT HIM, TRYING TO THINK ABOUT WHAT SHE HAD SAID THAT MIGHT CAUSE HIM TO LAUGH.

"I DON'T SUPPOSE YOU'RE GOING TO TELL ME WHAT WE'LL BE DOING AT THIS 'SAFE HOUSE' FOR THE NEXT THREE WEEKS?" SHE ASKED. "AFTER ALL, IT DOESN'T TAKE LONG TO GET TO BOSTON. AND FROM THERE NEW YORK ISN'T FAR."

HIS SMIRK WIDENED.

"I COULD TELL YOU," HE SAID. "BUT THAT WOULD SPOIL THE SURPRISE."

"YEAH, MY LIFE SEEMS FULL OF SURPRISES AT THE MOMENT," ANDI MUTTERED.

"YOU'RE NOT ALONE IN THAT," HE SAID.

HE WAS STILL WEARING THAT DAMNABLE, ARROGANT SMIRK. NOT TO MENTION THE TONE WITH WHICH HE HAD SAID THIS LAST BIT MADE IT SOUND AS THOUGH HE WAS NOT THE LEAST BIT HAPPY ABOUT THE PROSPECT OF BEING MATED TO HER.

SHE TRIED TO RECONCILE THIS WITH WHAT SHE'D HEARD IN THE HALLWAY. BUT, TRY AS SHE MIGHT, IT SEEMED IMPOSSIBLE. INSTEAD, SHE ASSUMED, OR AT LEAST TRIED TO ASSUME, HER OWN SUPERIOR SMIRK AND LOOKED HIM UP AND DOWN WITH FEIGNED DISTASTE.

AS HE WAS WEARING A WHITE T-SHIRT THAT WAS A GOOD BIT TIGHTER THAN ANYTHING SHE HAD SEEN HIM WEAR BEFORE AND SHOWED NEARLY EVERY INCH OF HIS SLENDER BUT WELL-TONED ABDOMEN, TRYING TO APPEAR UNINTERESTED WAS PROVING MUCH MORE DIFFICULT THAN SHE'D HOPED.

"SO," SHE SAID TRYING TO KEEP UP THE UNPHASED FACADE. "IS THERE ANYTHING YOU CAN TELL ME?"

"ABOUT WHAT?" HE ASKED.

"ABOUT ANYTHING," SHE SAID. "BUT, I GUESS WE COULD START WITH YOU."

"WHAT DO YOU WANT TO KNOW?"

ANDI HAD TO STOP AND THINK ABOUT THAT. THERE WERE A MILLION THINGS SHE WANTED TO KNOW ABOUT SETH. SHE WANTED TO KNOW WHAT THAT FEELING WAS THAT HE GOT WHEN HE SAW HER. SHE WANTED TO KNOW WHAT IT MEANT. SHE WANTED TO

58

KNOW WHY, IF HE WAS AS ATTRACTED TO HER AS HE'D TOLD HIS MOTHER HE WAS, HE'D BARELY SPOKEN TO HER IN THE TWO DAYS SINCE PETE HAD INTRODUCED THEM.

BUT, ASKING ANY OF THAT WAS OUT OF THE QUESTION. IT WOULD FORCE HER TO ADMIT THAT SHE'D OVERHEARD THE CONVERSATION BETWEEN HIM AND HIS MOTHER FOR ONE THING. AND SHE DIDN'T WANT SETH TO THINK THAT SHE WAS QUITE THAT NOSY.

SO, SHE GRASPED THE FIRST AND MOST OBVIOUS QUESTION THAT CAME TO MIND.

"HOW DID YOU BECOME A VAMPIRE?"

"DID...DID MATTHIAS...BITE YOU?" SHE ASKED. HE LOOKED UP AT HER WITH A SHARP LOOK THAT MADE HER IMMEDIATELY REGRET HAVING ASKED.

"SORRY," ANDI SAID. "I JUST…"

"NO, IT'S FINE," HE SAID SLOWLY. "GUESS YOU'VE GOT THE RIGHT TO KNOW. MATTATHIAS SAVED MY LIFE."

"HOW DID THAT HAPPEN?"

HE LOOKED UP AT HER, HIS EYES NOW WARRY INSTEAD OF ARROGANT OR SUPERIOR.

HE LOOKED AWAY SLOWLY AND TURNED HIS EYES TOWARDS THE WINDOW WHERE THE SUN HAD SET AND THE FIRST STARS WERE BEGINNING TO PEAK THROUGH THE LEAVES OF THE TALL TREES.

"IT HAPPENED HERE," HE SAID. "WE WEREN'T SUPPOSED TO GO INTO THE WOODS. MY PA WAS ALWAYS CLEAR ABOUT THAT. BUT, MY BROTHER DARED ME. THAT WAS WHEN I CAME UPON THE STRIGA."

"THOSE...THINGS IN THE CLUB...ATTACKED YOU?" ANDI ASKED. SHE IMAGINED THE GREAT, BAT-LIKE CREATURE THAT HAD FLOWN PAST HER JUST ONE NIGHT BEFORE. SOMEHOW, IT SEEMED MORE AT HOME IN THE WOODLAND OUTSIDE THAN IT DID IN THAT BRIGHT CLUB WITH THROBBING MUSIC AND SCANTILY DRESSED, SWEATY BODIES.

"YES," SETH SAID SOFTLY. "CLARA, THE WOMAN I CALL MY MOTHER, FOUND ME. SHE BROUGHT ME TO MATTATHIAS. HE REALIZED THAT I WOULDN'T SURVIVE THE WOUNDS I'D SUFFERED UNLESS HE TURNED ME."

"SO HE DID," SHE SAID UNNECESSARILY.

"HE DID," HE SAID. "AND THAT'S HOW I BECAME..LIKE THIS."

"SO...YOUR MOM AND MATTATHIAS, YOUR

DAD….THEY'RE NOT REALLY YOUR PARENTS?"

HE LOOKED UP AT HER SHARPLY AGAIN AS THOUGH THIS WERE A VERY IMPERTINENT QUESTION. THIS TIME, ANDI HAD NO DESIRE TO APOLOGIZE. AFTER ALL, IF SHE WAS GOING TO SPEND THE REST OF HER LIFE WITH THIS MAN, SHE HAD THE RIGHT TO KNOW AS MUCH ABOUT HIM AS POSSIBLE. AND HIS ATTEMPT TO HIDE THINGS FROM HER, AS SHE WAS SURE HE WAS DOING, DIDN'T EXACTLY PUT HER IN A GREAT MOOD.

"YOU KNOW WHAT I MEAN," SHE SAID DEFENSIVELY. "I MEAN…CLARA DIDN'T GIVE BIRTH TO YOU, DID SHE?"

"SHE'S MY MOTHER," SETH SAID EQUALLY DEFENSIVE. "BUT…NO. SHE DIDN'T GIVE BIRTH TO ME."

HE LOOKED DOWN AT HIS HANDS AS THOUGH LOST IN THOUGHT. ANDI WANTED TO ASK HIM A MILLION OTHER QUESTIONS. WHO WERE HIS FIRST PARENTS? WHY WAS HE SO QUICK TO DISMISS THEM? HE'D TALKED ABOUT A BROTHER, WHAT HAD HAPPENED TO HIM?

AS SOON AS SHE OPENED HER MOUTH TO ASK ANOTHER QUESTION, SETH STOOD QUICKLY FROM THE BED.

"WE'LL HEAD OUT IN TWENTY MINUTES,"

HE SAID AS HE MARCHED TOWARDS THE DOOR, REFUSING TO LOOK AT HER. "MOM'S PACKED SOME CLOTHES AND THINGS FOR YOU. WE'VE GOT TWO CARS READY OUTSIDE."

ANDI FOLLOWED HIM TO THE DOOR AND, NOT KNOWING QUITE WHAT SHE WAS DOING, REACHED A HAND OUT TO TOUCH HIS ARM AS HE OPENED IT.

HE STOPPED AT HER TOUCH AND SHE FELT HIM STIFFEN, FIRM MUSCLES TIGHTENING BENEATH THE COLD SKIN IN HER HAND.

"HEY, THANKS," SHE SAID. "YOU KNOW. FOR THE CLOTHES AND STUFF."

HE TURNED, HIS GRAY EYES MET HER GREEN ONES AND, FOR A MOMENT, ANDI SAW A FLASH OF SOMETHING BOTH FASCINATING AND DARK DART THROUGH HIS EYES.

A SHIVER RAN DOWN HER SPINE AND A WEIRD JUMPING SENSATION FILLED HER STOMACH. FOR THE FIRST TIME, SHE SAW IN THIS, RESERVED, STUCK UP YOUNG MAN, A HINT OF THE DEEP PASSION SHE'D OVERHEARD HIM SPEAKING ABOUT TO HIS MOTHER.

IN A MOMENT, HOWEVER, THE LOOK WAS GONE. HE MOVED HIS ARM OUT OF HER GRASP AND HIS SUPERIOR EXPRESSION RETURNED.

"DON'T THANK ME," HE SAID. "MOM GOT YOU THE CLOTHES. I'M JUST THE MESSENGER. BE READY IN TWENTY MINUTES."

SHE OPENED HER MOUTH TO RESPOND BUT, BEFORE SHE COULD, SETH HAD ALREADY TURNED ON HIS HEEL AND BEGAN TO MARCH AT A QUICK GAIT DOWN THE HALL.

ANDI STARED AFTER HIM, SURPRISE AT HIS QUICK CHANGE IN DEMEANOR FROM THAT STRANGE FLASH OF DESIRE TO THE COLD, INDIFFERENCE WAS QUICKLY REPLACED BY ANGER AND FRUSTRATION. SHE LET OUT A HUFF TO VOICE HER DISPLEASURE AND SLAMMED THE DOOR TO SHOW THE SAME.

SO, HE WANTED TO KEEP HER IN THE DARK ABOUT EVERYTHING IMPORTANT? HE WANTED TO TREAT HER LIKE SHE WAS SOME KIND OF...BUG...HE HAD TO PUT UP WITH EVEN THOUGH HE DIDN'T WANT TO?

WELL, THAT WAS JUST FINE WITH HER. AFTER ALL, THIS MATING WASN'T ABOUT HER OR SETH. IT WAS ABOUT SAVING THE WORLD. AND THAT DIDN'T REQUIRE KNOWING OR EVEN LIKING THE GUY SHE WAS GOING TO BE MATED TO.

BUT, AS SHE ANGRILY BRUSHED HER HAIR WITH THE COMB AT HER VANITY, SHE

REALIZED THAT, REALLY, IT WASN'T FINE WITH HER. THE MORE SHE TALKED TO SETH, THE MORE SHE WANTED TO KNOW ABOUT HIM. AND, DESPITE HER HABIT OF MAKING OUT WITH GUYS IN CLUBS WHEN SHE'D HAD A FEW WHITE RUSSIANS, SHE'D NEVER GONE TO BED WITH A GUY SHE DIDN'T LIKE OR AT LEAST KNOW WELL.

AND, WHAT'S MORE, SHE KNEW THAT SHE WOULDN'T BE ABLE TO. NO MATTER HOW MUCH THE FATE OF HUMANITY DEPENDED ON IT.

NO, SHE REALIZED, SHE WOULD HAVE TO GET TO KNOW SETH KILLGORE. AND, SHE DECIDED FIRMLY, SHE WOULD, WHETHER HE LIKED IT OR NOT.

AFTER ALL, AS ANDI HAD ONCE TOLD SETH, SHE WASN'T ONE TO GIVE UP.

Chapter Four

"SO, IS IT TRUE THAT VAMPIRES CAN'T SEE THEIR REFLECTIONS?"

"NO," SETH SAID SIMPLY.

"NO, THEY CAN'T SEE THEIR REFLECTIONS OR NO IT'S NOT TRUE THAT THEY CAN'T?" ANDI ASKED.

SETH HEAVED A SIGH AS THOUGH THOROUGHLY IRRITATED.

"I CAN SEE MY REFLECTION," HE SAID.

THEY'D BEEN DRIVING FOR ABOUT TWENTY MINUTES AND IT WAS THE MOST HE'D SAID TO HER IN ALL THAT TIME. ANDI TRIED TO CONVINCE HERSELF THAT IT WAS PROGRESS BUT, SHE COULDN'T HELP BUT BE MORE THAN A BIT DISCOURAGED.

"I WONDER HOW THAT RUMOR GOT STARTED," SHE SAID.

"WOULDN'T KNOW," HE ANSWERED. SHE LOOKED OVER AT HIM HOPEFULLY, THINKING THAT HE JUST MIGHT ELABORATE. HE DIDN'T.

WITH A HUFF, ANDI THREW HERSELF BACK INTO THE CHAIR AND GLARED AT THE LITTLE CLOCK ON THE DASHBOARD. TEN THIRTY. PETER HAD EXPLAINED TO HER THAT THEY WOULD BE TAKING THE BACKROADS TO BOSTON AND WOULD BE DOING A LOT OF DOUBLE BACKING IN CASE ANYONE CONNECTED WITH THE STRIGA WAS FOLLOWING THEM.

"APPARENTLY, THEY KNOW ABOUT YOU NOW," PETER SAID. "THEY'LL BE ON YOUR TAIL. AND OURS TOO BY DEFAULT."

THAT MEANT THEY WOULDN'T REACH THE SAFE HOUSE UNTIL AFTER MIDNIGHT. MAYBE ONE OR TWO O'CLOCK IN THE MORNING. THAT MEANT TWO OR THREE HOURS STUCK IN A CAR WITH NO ONE BUT THE STONE-FACED SETH KILLGORE FOR A COMPANY.

PETER AND CAIN WERE DRIVING BEHIND THEM. "COVERING YOUR BACK" AS CAIN PUT IT.

"BESIDES," CAIN HAD SAID TEASINGLY. "YOU LOVEBIRDS NEED TO GET USED TO SPENDING TIME TOGETHER."

A FLUSH HAD COME INTO SETH'S FACE AT THAT AND HE'D BRUSHED HIS BROTHER OFF. HE HADN'T SAID MUCH SINCE THEN, DESPITE ANDI'S INCREASINGLY DESPERATE ATTEMPTS AT CONVERSATION.

"WHAT'S THAT?" ANDI ASKED, HER EYES CATCHING ON A STRANGE LOOKING BLACK RADIO ON THE CAR'S DASH.

"RADIO," SETH SAID.

"BUT, IT'S NOT A NORMAL RADIO, IS IT?" SHE ASKED.

"IT'S A POLICE RADIO," HE SAID. "IT'S HOW WE HUNT."

"WHAT DO YOU MEAN HOW YOU HUNT?"

HE ROLLED HIS EYES AND HEAVED A SIGH AS THOUGH HE WAS ABOUT TO TELL HER SOMETHING AGAINST HIS BETTER JUDGMENT.

"WE'RE SUPPOSED TO BE 'ANGELS OF VENGEANCE'. THAT'S WHAT THE PACT SAYS," HE TOLD HER. "SO, WHEN WE'RE RUNNING LOW ON...FOOD...WE LISTEN TO THE RADIO FOR THINGS LIKE CHRONIC DOMESTIC ABUSE, SERIAL KILLERS, KNOWN PEDOPHILES THAT KIND OF THING. WE FIND THE PEOPLE WHO'VE COMMITTED THOSE CRIMES AND WE...USE THEIR BLOOD."

"KIND OF LIKE A DEXTER THING," SHE SAID IN UNDERSTANDING.

"DEXTER?" HE ASKED LOOKING AT HER, FOR THE FIRST TIME, HE SEEMED A BIT

CURIOUS.

"IT'S A TV SHOW," SHE SAID. "HE'S A SERIAL KILLER WHO ONLY KILLS SERIAL KILLERS."

HE GAVE HER HALF A SMILE WHICH, ACTUALLY, MADE HIM LOOK MORE PLEASANT THAN USUAL.

"YEAH, SOMETHING LIKE THAT."

THE SMILE LINGERED FOR A MOMENT. PERHAPS IT WAS THAT WHICH MADE HER WANT TO KNOW SOMETHING ELSE. SOMETHING MORE ABOUT THIS MAN SHE WAS DESTINED TO MARRY.

"SO...HOW DOES THAT AGE THING WORK?" SHE ASKED. "I MEAN, YOU SAID YOU WERE BITTEN WHAT? TWO HUNDRED YEARS AGO? YOU WERE ELEVEN OR TWELVE? NOW YOU'RE..."

"TWENTY," HE SAID. "OR...I APPEAR TO BE. I AGE EVERY TWENTY-FIVE YEARS INSTEAD OF EVERY ONE."

"OH," ANDI SAID. "SO YOU'RE REALLY...TWO HUNDRED AND TWELVE YEARS OLD?"

"YES," SETH SAID STIFFLY.

"ABOUT HOW LONG DO VAMPIRES LIVE,

THEN?"

"ABOUT EIGHT HUNDRED YEARS," HE SAID. "SOME ONE THOUSAND."

"SO IS YOUR DAD...MATTATHIAS, LIKE...?"

"ABOUT FIVE HUNDRED YEARS OLD," HE SAID. "HE LOOKS ABOUT FIFTY."

"BUT," ANDI SAID THINKING QUICKLY. "IF CLARA...I MEAN...YOUR MOM...SHE'S HUMAN!"

"THAT'S RIGHT," HE SAID.

"BUT SHE WAS THERE WHEN YOU WERE BITTEN?"

"YES," HE ANSWERED. SHE WAITED AGAIN FOR HIM TO ELABORATE HE DIDN'T SEEM INCLINED TO.

"WELL?" ANDI ASKED FRUSTRATED. "ARE YOU GOING TO TELL ME HOW THAT WORKS?"

"DO YOU WANT TO KNOW?"

"IF I DIDN'T, I WOULDN'T HAVE ASKED," SHE SAID ARMS FOLDED ACROSS HER CHEST.

"YOU'LL DRINK SOMETHING AT THE MATING," HE SAID FINALLY. HE SOUNDED AS THOUGH HE WAS BEING PRESSURED TO

ANSWER AGAINST HIS BETTER JUDGMENT. "IT'LL SLOW YOUR AGING TO MATCH WITH MINE. THAT WAY WE HAVE A CHANCE TO LIVE ALONGSIDE ONE ANOTHER."

"WHAT DO I DRINK?"

"DON'T WORRY ABOUT IT," HE SAID. "YOU'LL FIND OUT WHEN YOU GET THERE."

"WHAT IF I'D LIKE TO KNOW NOW?"

"YOU'LL HAVE TO GET USED TO DISAPPOINTMENT," HE SAID.

ANOTHER FRUSTRATED FLARE ROSE UP IN HER CHEST. THE FRUSTRATION TURNED TO ANGER WHEN SHE SAW THAT HE WAS, ONCE MORE, SMIRKING. AS THOUGH HE WAS LAUGHING AT HER. THOUGH, SHE REALLY DIDN'T KNOW WHY WANTING TO KNOW ABOUT WHAT WAS ABOUT TO HAPPEN TO HER MADE HER SO RIDICULOUS IN HIS EYES.

"FINE," SHE SAID BITTERLY. "DON'T TELL ME."

"WASN'T PLANNING ON IT," HE SAID AS THOUGH PLEASED THAT SHE HAD FINALLY COME AROUND TO SEEING THINGS HIS WAY.

ANDI SAT IN STONY SILENCE FOR ANOTHER FIFTEEN MINUTES. DETERMINED TO PUNISH

HIM FOR HIS REFUSAL TO GIVE HER ANYTHING MORE THAN SHORT, CLIPPED RESPONSES.

BUT, SHE WAS BOTH ASTOUNDED AND SURPRISED TO FIND THAT HE DIDN'T SEEM ANGRY OR UPSET BY HER SILENCE AT ALL. INDEED, HE KEPT GLANCING AT HER WITH HALF A SMILE ON HIS LIPS AS THOUGH HE THOUGHT HER GLARES OF ANGER AMUSING OR CUTE.

WELL, IF HE WAS HAPPY IN SILENCE, SHE SUPPOSED SHE SHOULD TRY TO FORCE HIM TO TALK AGAIN. THAT SEEMED TO ANNOY HIM. AND, IF SHE WAS GOING TO BE ANNOYED THEN HE WAS SURE AS WELL GOING TO BE ANNOYED TOO.

"YOU KNOW I'M A LITTLE SURPRISED AT YOU," SHE SAID IN HER MOST TANTALIZING VOICE. HOPING TO GET HIM TO ASK WHY SHE WAS SURPRISED. THOUGH, SHE SUPPOSED THAT WAS SOMETHING OF A PIPE DREAM NOW. AS SHE SHOULD HAVE PREDICTED, SETH MERELY GLANCED AT HER ANOTHER HALF SMIRK ON HIS LIPS.

"DO YOU WANT TO KNOW WHY I'M SURPRISED?"

"NOT REALLY," HE SAID. "BUT, I'VE GOT A FEELING YOU'LL TELL ME ANYWAY."

THE FRUSTRATED SURGE IN ANDI'S STOMACH COLORED HER NEXT WORDS.

"SEE, THAT'S THE PROBLEM WITH YOU! YOU DON'T EVEN HAVE A...A HINT OF CURIOSITY! DON'T YOU WANT TO KNOW ANYTHING ABOUT ME AT ALL?"

"THAT DEPENDS," HE SAID. THAT STUPID LITTLE SMILE STILL ON HIS LIPS. "WHAT DO YOU WANT TO TELL ME?"

HE GLANCED AT HER AND HIS GRIN WIDENED TO PLACE A SHIMMERING LIGHT IN HIS EYES. ANDI WOULD HAVE THOUGHT IT PARTICULARLY ATTRACTIVE HAD SHE NOT BEEN SO FURIOUS WITH HIM. WHY DID HE HAVE TO BE SO HOT AND SO INFURIATING AT THE SAME TIME?

"IF YOU DON'T WANT TO KNOW, WHY SHOULD I TELL YOU?" SHE ASKED.

SHE FOLDED HER ARMS ACROSS HER CHEST AGAIN AND BECAME DETERMINED NOT TO SPEAK AGAIN UNTIL HE DID. THOUGH TRUTH BE TOLD, AS THE SILENCE STRETCHED ON, SHE WASN'T SURE JUST HOW LONG SHE WOULD BE ABLE TO HOLD OUT. SHE'D NEVER LIKED SILENCE MUCH. IT WAS ESPECIALLY BAD WHEN THAT SILENCE WAS AWKWARD.

AFTER ONLY FIVE MINUTES, ANDI WAS

ALREADY THINKING OF SOMETHING ELSE SHE COULD ASK HER CAR MATE. BUT, BEFORE SHE COULD, SHE WAS SURPRISED TO FIND HIM SPEAKING.

"ACTUALLY, THERE IS SOMETHING I WANT TO KNOW ABOUT YOU," HE SAID.

"WHAT?" SHE ASKED.

"WHY DIDN'T YOU TELL ME YOU WERE LISTENING AT THE DOOR WHEN I WAS TALKING TO MY MOTHER."

ANDI FELT HER FACE FLUSH AND HER JAW FALL SLIGHTLY TO THE FLOOR.

"YOU...YOU KNEW I WAS LISTENING?"

"VAMPIRES HAVE HEIGHTENED SENSES. LITTLE KNOWN FACT," HE SAID.

"REALLY?"

"NO. YOUR FEET ARE REALLY LOUD. I COULD HEAR THE FLOORBOARDS CREAKING."

ANDI FELT, EVEN MORE, BLOOD RUSH TO HER FACE AND SHE TRIED HER BEST TO GLARE AT HIM. THOUGH, AS HIS EYES WERE ON THE ROAD, HE DIDN'T SEEM TO NOTICE.

"SO, WHY DIDN'T YOU SAY ANYTHING?" HE

ASKED.

"I...I THOUGHT IT WAS TOO PERSONAL," SHE SAID.

"NEVER STOPPED YOU BEFORE," HE ANSWERED. "YOU WERE THE ONE WHO WANTED TO KNOW EVERYTHING ABOUT ME."

HE GLANCED AT HER AND SHE LOOKED DOWN AT HER FEET BITING HER LIP.

"I...I GUESS," SHE STARTED REALIZING SHE WOULD HAVE TO TELL HIM THE TRUTH. "I GUESS...I MEAN YOU ALREADY DON'T LIKE ME. I THOUGHT IT WOULD BE WORSE IF YOU THOUGHT I WAS SPYING ON YOU."

SHE CHANCED TO GLANCE AT HIM EXPECTING TO SEE HIS ARROGANT SMILE ONCE MORE. INSTEAD, ALL HINT OF AMUSEMENT DISAPPEARED FROM HIS FACE. A SULLEN GLOWER REPLACED IT AS HE KEPT HIS EYES FIXED EVEN MORE FIRMLY ON THE ROAD.

"YOU KNOW," HE SAID AFTER FIVE MINUTES AWKWARD SILENCE. "I WISH YOU'D LET ME EARN YOUR LOW OPINION OF ME. IT'S MORE FUN THAT WAY."
"WHAT DO YOU MEAN MY LOW OPINION OF YOU?" SHE ASKED NOW MORE SURPRISED THAN ANGRY OR FRUSTRATED.

"I MEAN YOU AUTOMATICALLY ASSUME THE WORST ABOUT ME," HE SAID. "WHAT WOULD MAKE YOU THINK I DON'T LIKE YOU?"

"YOU'RE...ALWAYS LAUGHING AT ME."

SHE SAW HIM GIVE A SMALL EYE ROLL BEFORE GLANCING AT HER ONCE MORE.

"DID YOU EVER CONSIDER THAT I MIGHT BE LAUGHING BECAUSE I THINK YOU'RE FUNNY?" HE ASKED.

HER EYES WIDENED AND SHE TRIED HER BEST TO COME UP WITH AN ANSWER THAT WOULDN'T MAKE HER SEEM LIKE EVEN MORE OF AN IDIOT.

"SEE?" HE SAID. "LOW OPINION."

SHE TRIED ONCE AGAIN TO THINK OF SOME
KIND OF APOLOGY OR EXPLANATION. BUT,
THE LONGER SHE LEFT IT, THE ODDER IT
WOULD SEEM.

SO, INSTEAD, SHE LOOKED OUT THE
WINDOW AND TRIED TO FIND SOMETHING,
ANYTHING THAT SHE COULD TALK ABOUT
INSTEAD. FINALLY, ON ONE OF THE BACK
LANES, SHE SAW A LARGE MCDONALDS SIGN
ONLY HALF LIT UP IN THE NIGHT.

"YOU KNOW, I'VE SEEN A LOT OF THOSE,"
SHE SAID.

"MCDONALD'S SIGNS? SO HAVE I."

"I MEAN ONES THAT ARE ONLY HALF LIT
UP," SHE SAID WITH AN EYE ROLL. "YOU'D
THINK A BIG OUTFIT LIKE MCDONALDS WOULD
BE ABLE TO AFFORD DECENT SIGNAGE."

"WHEN IT'S ONLY HALF LIT UP LIKE THAT IT
MEANS THAT THE RESTAURANT'S CLOSED BUT
THE DRIVE THROUGH'S STILL OPEN," HE SAID.

"REALLY?"

"NO."

SHE ROLLED HER EYES AT HIM BUT, FOUND
HERSELF SMILING AND MUCH LESS
FRUSTRATED THAN SHE HAD BEEN WHEN
THEY FIRST SET OUT. MAYBE IT WOULDN'T BE
SUCH A LONG DRIVE AFTER ALL.

Chapter Five

THEY REACHED WHAT SETH HAD CALLED
THE "SAFE HOUSE" WHICH TURNED OUT TO BE
AN OLD AND ALLEGEDLY ABANDONED HOUSE
JUST OUTSIDE THE CITY LIMITS.

ANDI WAS MORE THAN SURPRISED BY THE
RAMSHACKLE STRUCTURE. ESPECIALLY WHEN
SHE COMPARED THIS DRAB BUILDING TO THE
LUXURY OF WOODHOUSE.

"THAT'S WHY THEY CALL IT A SAFE HOUSE,"
CAIN TOLD HER WHEN HE, ANDI AND PETER,
LED BY SETH MADE THEIR WAY INSIDE. "NO
ONE'D THINK THAT WE VAMPIR WOULD
CHOOSE TO STAY IN THIS LITTLE PLACE.
ESPECIALLY NOT FOR WEEKS ON END."

"WEEKS?" ANDI ASKED AS THEY ENTERED
THE SPACE. IT WAS NOT MUCH LARGER THAN A
STUDIO APARTMENT AND MUCH MORE BARE.
THE LIGHTING WAS DIM, EVEN WHEN SETH
TURNED ON THE LIGHTS, AND THE FURNITURE
WAS RAGGED AND VERY WELL WORN.

"I THOUGHT THIS WAS JUST GOING TO BE
AN OVERNIGHT THING."

LOOKING AROUND AT THIS DREARY LITTLE SPOT SHE TRIED AND FAILED TO IMAGINE HERSELF HOLED UP INSIDE IT FOR MORE THAN ONE NIGHT. ESPECIALLY WITHOUT ACCESS TO THE OUTSIDE WORLD.

"WE'VE GOT TO LAY LOW HERE UNTIL JUST TWO DAYS BEFORE THE CEREMONY," PETER SAID.

"WHY?" ANDI ASKED.

"BECAUSE THE STRIGA KNOW YOU TWO ARE TOGETHER," CAIN ANSWERED. HIS TONE WAS MUCH MORE NONCHALANT THAN ANDI WOULD HAVE EXPECTED GIVEN THE CIRCUMSTANCES. "THAT MEANS THEY'LL BE SEARCHING FOR YOUR SCENT."

"I THOUGHT YOU SAID VAMPIRES DIDN'T HAVE HEIGHTENED SENSES," ANDI SAID TURNING ACCUSINGLY TO SETH.

"VAMPIR DON'T," SETH SAID. "BUT, STRIGA ARE DIFFERENT. THEY...THEY'VE MADE A CONTRACT WITH EVIL. THAT'S WHY THEY'RE STRONGER THAN US."

"YEAH," CAIN SAID CASUALLY. "PAIN IN THE ASS BUT, IT MEANS THAT YOU TWO CAN'T GO OUT FOR THE NEXT FEW WEEKS. AT LEAST NOT TOGETHER. AND DEFINITELY NOT TO THE HOUSE IN NEW YORK. THAT WOULD LEAD THE

STRIGA STRAIGHT TO HEADQUARTERS."

ANDI HAD A MILLION MORE QUESTIONS BUT, FOR THE FIRST TIME THAT EVENING, SHE REALIZED JUST HOW EXHAUSTING HER CURIOSITY COULD BE. NOW, STANDING ON HER FEET AFTER HOURS SITTING IN A CAR, SHE COULD BARELY KEEP HER EYES OPEN.

STILL, SHE TRIED TO BLINK THE SLEEP AWAY. APPARENTLY, SETH, AT THE VERY LEAST, WASN'T FOOLED.

"YOU SHOULD SLEEP," HE SAID. HE MOVED TOWARDS HER AND SHE FOUGHT DOWN A FLUTTER OF BUTTERFLIES IN HER STOMACH WHEN HE PUT AN ARM FIRMLY AROUND HER SHOULDER AND POINTED HER TOWARDS A DOOR ON THE OTHER SIDE OF THE SMALL ROOM.

"I'LL SHOW YOU WHERE YOU'LL SLEEP," HE SAID.

"YOU MEAN THERE'S MORE THAN ONE ROOM IN THIS ROACH MOTEL?" SHE ASKED.

"JUST ONE OTHER ONE," SETH SAID. "IT'S FOR YOU."

"BUT, IF YOU GET SCARED AT NIGHT AND WANT SETH TO GO IN AND SLEEP WITH YOU, WE WON'T MIND," CAIN CALLED CHEEKILY. "IN

81

FACT, I'LL VOLUNTEER IF HE'S NOT WILLING."

ANDI LOOKED OVER HER SHOULDER AND SAW HIM THROW HER A WINK.

"I'VE SEEN THE WAY YOU DANCE. I THINK I'LL PASS," SHE SAID DRYLY. EVEN THOUGH SHE'D THROWN THIS TEASING LINE TO HIM, SHE COULD FEEL A HINT OF BLOOD FLOOD HER CHEEKS. SHE STILL REMEMBERED THE CONVERSATION SHE'D HEARD ABOUT SETH AND CAIN AND SUCCESSION, AFTER ALL.

"I'M AN AMAZING DANCER," HE SAID PRETENDING TO BE SHOCKED. "YOU JUST WON'T ADMIT IT TO YOURSELF."

"GO ON AND UNPACK. BOTH OF YOU," SETH SAID TURNING, SUDDENLY STERN TO BOTH HIS BROTHER AND PETE. CAIN LOOKED AT SETH, THE SMILE FADING FROM HIS FACE. HE SEEMED ABOUT TO SAY SOMETHING BUT, BEFORE HE COULD PETER GRABBED HIM GENTLY BY THE ARM AND TOOK HIM OUT OF ANDI AND SETH'S LINE OF VISION.

"SORRY ABOUT THAT," SETH SAID. "I PROMISE YOU WON'T HAVE TO PUT UP WITH HIM TOO MUCH THESE NEXT FEW WEEKS."

"NO, YOU'RE THE ONE WHO GETS THAT PLEASURE," SHE SAID. "AND I HONESTLY WISH YOU LUCK WITH THAT."

"I'M USED TO IT," HE SAID. THAT LITTLE SMIRK REAPPEARED ON HIS LIPS. THOUGH TRUTH BE TOLD, IT SEEMED A TAD LESS ARROGANT NOW. MAYBE IT WAS THE LIGHTING, MAYBE IT WAS THE WAY HIS GRAY EYES LIT UP AND STARTED TO SPARKLE IN A WAY SHE HADN'T NOTICED BEFORE. EITHER WAY, SOMETHING WAS CERTAINLY DIFFERENT.

THERE WAS ALSO SOMETHING DIFFERENT IN THE WAY THEY STOOD AT THE DOORWAY TO HER ROOM, AWKWARDLY LOOKING AT EACH OTHER THEN GLANCING AWAY AS THOUGH THEY WERE TWO HIGH SCHOOLERS JUST COMING HOME FROM A FIRST DATE.

"I'LL...ER...I'LL JUST BE OUT HERE IF YOU...IF YOU NEED ANYTHING," HE SAID.

"THANKS," SHE SAID. "I DOUBT I'LL DO MUCH OTHER THAN SLEEP. HAVEN'T DONE MUCH OF THAT IN THE LAST FORTY EIGHT HOURS."

"I GUESS NOT."

AN AWKWARD PAUSE PASSED BETWEEN THEM. BEFORE SHE COULD THINK OF SOMETHING TO FILL IT HE SUDDENLY REACHED DOWN AND GRABBED HER HAND IN HIS.

HER BREATH CAUGHT IN HER THROAT AS SETH TOOK HER HAND AND BROUGHT THE BACK OF IT TO HIS LIPS. PLACING A GENTLE KISS ON HER KNUCKLES.

THE STRANDS OF HIS DARK HAIR BRUSHED HER SKIN AS HIS EYES LOOKED BACK UP AT HER.

"SORRY," HE SAID QUIETLY. "THAT'S JUST...IT'S SOMETHING I'VE SEEN MY DAD DO."

"DON'T APOLOGIZE," ANDI SAID. "IT'S NICE."

THE SMILE THAT LIT HIS FACE WAS BRIGHTER THAN ANY SHE HAD YET SEEN HIM WEAR AND IT WAS ENOUGH TO CAUSE HIM TO FLOAT IN AND OUT OF HER DREAMS AGAIN THAT NIGHT. THOUGH, THIS TIME, THEY WERE ALL MUCH MORE PLEASANT.

WHAT WASN'T PLEASANT, AT LEAST NOT ENTIRELY, WAS STAYING COOPED UP IN A BLAND LITTLE BOX DAY AND NIGHT FOR NEARLY TWO WEEKS.

AT SETH'S INSISTENCE, OVER THE NEXT TWO WEEKS, ANDI WASN'T ALLOWED TO LEAVE THE SAFE HOUSE AT ALL. NOT TO GET FOOD, NOT TO GET THE MAIL, NOT EVEN JUST TO STAND OUTSIDE IN THE SUNLIGHT FOR FIVE MINUTES SO THAT SHE COULD FEEL LIKE A NORMAL HUMAN BEING. HE SAID IT WAS TOO

RISKY. A POINT ON WHICH PETER AND CAIN
SEEMED TO AGREE.

WELL, ANDI THOUGHT, IF HE WAS A LITTLE
OVERPROTECTIVE, HE WAS AT LEAST FAIR
ABOUT IT. HE NEVER LEFT THE SAFE HOUSE
EITHER. AND PETER DID ONLY BRIEFLY.
USUALLY AT NIGHT.

CAIN WAS THE ONE WHO WENT OUT
FREQUENTLY TO FETCH FOOD FOR HER AND
PETER AND TO BRING ALL OF THEM NEWS
ABOUT WHAT WAS HAPPENING ON THE
OUTSIDE. APPARENTLY, THERE HADN'T BEEN
ANY MORE SIGHTINGS OF THE STRIGA,
THOUGH MATTATHIAS KNEW THEY WERE STILL
THERE, BIDDING THEIR TIME.

"DAD TELLS US NOT TO TRUST ANYONE,"
CAIN SAID, RETURNING FROM ONE OF HIS
NIGHTLY OUTINGS. "BUT, THEN, DAD ALWAYS
SAYS THAT. HE'S PARANOID."

"HE'S ALSO NOT DEAD," SETH REMINDED
HIS YOUNGER BROTHER. CAIN ONLY GAVE A
NON COMMITTAL SHRUG AT THIS GENTLE
REBUKE. WHICH CAUSED SETH TO TURN TO
ANDI AND GIVE HER A KNOWING EYE ROLL
WHICH SHE RETURNED.

ANOTHER GOOD THING ABOUT BEING
COOPED UP IN A HOUSE WITH SETH FOR TWO
WEEKS, SHE NOW KNEW MORE THAN SHE EVER
THOUGHT IT POSSIBLE TO KNOW ABOUT THE

85

MAN WHO WAS ABOUT TO BE HER HUSBAND OR
MATE OR...WHATEVER.

SHE KNEW HE'D ALWAYS BEEN CAUTIOUS,
EVEN AS A BOY. HE KNEW THAT HIS MIDDLE
BROTHER, JEREMIAH ALWAYS TEASED HIM FOR
BEING TOO BOOKISH AND TOO SENSITIVE.
THAT WAS WHY JEREMIAH HAD DARED HIM TO
GO INTO THE WOODS AND THAT WAS WHY
SETH HAD TAKEN THE DARE.

"I WANTED TO PROVE I WAS A MAN," SETH
SAID.

SHE KNEW HIS MOTHER DIED WHEN HE
WAS YOUNG. SHE ALSO KNEW THAT SET HIS
FATHER TO DRINKING.

"HE NEVER HAD TIME FOR ME AND MY
BROTHERS AFTER THAT," SETH SAID. "MY
OLDEST BROTHER, BENJAMIN, TRIED TO LOOK
AFTER JEREMIAH AND ME, BUT...HE WAS
MARRIED. HAD HIS OWN FAMILY."

THE SUBJECT OF FATHERS WAS A
PARTICULARLY SORE ONE FOR BOTH OF THEM.
SHE'D TOLD HIM ALL ABOUT HERS. PETER'S
UNCLE AND ANDI'S FATHER HAD ALWAYS BEEN
THE BLACK SHEEP OF THE COOKE FAMILY. HE
TOOK OFF WHEN ANDI WAS THREE AND NO
ONE HAD HEARD FROM HIM SINCE.

"ONCE I GOT A POSTCARD WITH A PICTURE

OF HIS FAVORITE KIND OF MOTORCYCLE ON IT," SHE TOLD HIM. "BUT, IT WASN'T SIGNED. SO, I CAN'T REALLY BE SURE IT WAS HIM."

THEY'D BOTH AGREED THAT FATHERS CAN SUCK SOMETIMES. THEY'D ALSO AGREED THAT BROTHERS CAN SUCK SOMETIMES. ANDI DIDN'T HAVE ANY OF THOSE. BUT, AS SHE'D SPENT HER SUMMERS WITH PETER AND HIS PARENTS EVERY YEAR SINCE SHE WAS TWO, HE WAS SORT OF THE SAME THING.

SETH AND ANDI HAD TALKED ABOUT A LOT OF THINGS OVER THE PAST FEW WEEKS. THEY'D DISCUSSED MOVIES, BOOKS, FAMILIES A LITTLE OF EVERYTHING AND A LITTLE OF NOTHING. THE ONE THING THEY HADN'T DISCUSSED WAS WHAT WOULD HAPPEN TO THEM ON THE NIGHT OF THE MATING.

ANDI STILL DIDN'T KNOW WHAT THE CEREMONY ENTAILED. SHE'D TRIED TO PRY IT OUT OF SETH ON THE FIRST WEEK AT THE SAFE HOUSE BUT, HE'D BLOWN HER OFF.

"IT'S HARD TO EXPLAIN," HE'D SAID. "YOU'LL SEE WHEN WE GET THERE."

NO MATTER HOW HARD SHE TRIED TO PRESS, THAT WAS ALL HE WOULD TELL HER. IT TURNED OUT THAT HE WAS EVERY BIT AS STUBBORN AS SHE WAS WHEN IT CAME TO THINGS HE DID AND DID NOT WANT TO TELL.

ANOTHER THING THEY HADN'T TALKED ABOUT WAS A NEW...SOMETHING...THAT WAS QUICKLY AND QUIETLY DEVELOPING BETWEEN THEM. SHE COULD FEEL IT NOW EVERY TIME HE LAUGHED AT A JOKE SHE TOLD OR WHEN HE MET HER EYES AND SHE GLANCED DOWN AT HER HANDS, SMILING LIGHTLY AS HER STOMACH PERFORMED BACK FLIPS.

HE KISSED HER HAND EVERY NIGHT NOW BEFORE SHE WENT TO BED. OFTEN, VERY OFTEN, SHE THOUGHT HE WANTED TO KISS MORE THAN HER HAND. BUT, EVERY NIGHT, HE LEFT IT AT THAT. AND, EVERY TIME SHE THOUGHT OF BRINGING IT UP, THE WORDS GOT CAUGHT AND WOULDN'T COME OUT.

SHE KNEW HE WOULD BE EMBARRASSED TO TALK ABOUT IT. IF THERE WAS ONE THING SHE'D LEARNED ABOUT SETH BEYOND ANYTHING ELSE, HE WAS A VERY PRIVATE PERSON. HE DIDN'T LIKE ANYONE TO SEE BEYOND HIS CONTROL FACADE. AND LOSING THAT CONTROL WAS ONE OF HIS WORST FEARS. ANDI THOUGHT IT WAS LUCKY FOR ALL OF THEM THAT HE NEVER DID.

UNTIL ONE NIGHT. ONE NIGHT WHEN, JUST AS SHE WAS LAYING DOWN TO GO TO SLEEP, SHE HEARD HIM LET OUT A CURSE SO LOUD SHE WORRIED THAT HE'D ALERTED HALF OF

BOSTON TO THEIR PRESENCE.

"IT'S GONE. HOW CAN IT BE GONE!"

SHE HEARD HIM SAY. SURPRISED AND MORE
THAN A LITTLE CURIOUS, ANDI PUT HER FEET
ON THE FLOOR AND PADDED OVER TO THE
DOOR OF HER BEDROOM JUST IN TIME TO
HEAR WHAT SOUNDED LIKE A FRIDGE DOOR
SLAM, RATTLING THE WALLS OF THE SMALL
SAFE HOUSE.

"WE PROBABLY JUST MISJUDGED HOW MUCH
YOU WOULD NEED," CAIN WAS SAYING. "IT'S
NOT A BIG DEAL."

"NOT A BIG DEAL?!"

SETH'S VOICE WAS SO LOUD THAT IT
SOUNDED TO ANDI AS THOUGH HE WAS RIGHT
NEXT TO HER RATHER THAN ON THE OTHER
SIDE OF A HARD CONCRETE SLAB.

"YOU KNOW WHAT HAPPENS WHEN I CAN'T
FEED!" HE SAID. "I NEED-"

"I KNOW!" CAIN SAID. "BUT, WE'VE GOT THE
POLICE RADIO I CAN GO HUNT SOMEONE
DOWN FOR YOU REALLY QUICK."

A CHARGED SILENCE FELL BETWEEN THE
TWO BROTHERS. IT LASTED LONG ENOUGH
THAT ANDI PRESSED HER EAR TO THE DOOR

WONDERING IF SHE HAD MISSED SOMETHING.

"I DON'T WANT TO BE LEFT ALONE HERE," SETH SAID. "NOT WITH HER. NOT WITHOUT-"

"DON'T WORRY," CAIN SAID. "SHE'S ASLEEP."

"THAT'S EVEN WORSE," SETH SAID.

A SIGH, LOUD ENOUGH TO BE HEARD EVEN THROUGH THE WALLS SOUNDED FROM THE ROOM. ANDI THOUGHT IT CAME FROM CAIN BUT SHE COULDN'T BE QUITE SURE.

"LOOK, THE SOONER I LEAVE, THE SOONER I'LL GET BACK," CAIN SAID. "AND, ANYWAY, ISN'T THAT PART OF THE MATING PROCESS OR WHATEVER? AREN'T YOU SUPPOSED TO WANT TO BITE HER, TO WANT TO DRINK HER BLOOD? AREN'T YOU SUPPOSED TO BE ABLE TO STOP YOURSELF?"

"WHAT IF I CAN'T?" SETH SAID QUIETLY.

"HAVE SOME FAITH IN YOURSELF," CAIN SAID. SHE HEARD HIM MAKE A SHUFFLING SOUND AS THOUGH MOVING TOWARDS THE DOOR.

"I'LL BE BACK AS SOON AS I CAN."

THE OUTSIDE DOOR CLICKED CLOSED. ANDI LISTENED AT THE DOOR ANOTHER

MINUTE, UNSURE WHAT SHE WAS LISTENING FOR. UNSURE WHAT, EXACTLY, TO THINK.

SHE THOUGHT SHE UNDERSTOOD NOW WHAT SETH HAD TALKED TO HIS MOTHER ABOUT. ABOUT THE DESIRE FOR ANDI, THE WANT OF HER THAT HE COULDN'T DO ANYTHING ABOUT.

SETH WANTED TO BITE HER. HE WANTED TO DRINK HER BLOOD.

ANDI KNEW THAT THIS REVELATION SHOULD HAVE SHOCKED HER OR MADE HER SICK TO HER STOMACH. INSTEAD, SHE WAS SURPRISED TO FIND THAT IT DIDN'T ENCOURAGE ANY STRONG FEELINGS AT ALL.SHE FELT AS THOUGH SHE HAD JUST LEARNED A MILDLY INTERESTING TRIVIA FACT. SOMETHING YOU WOULD USE TO IMPRESS YOUR FRIENDS BUT, NOTHING MORE THAN THAT.

MAYBE THIS LACK OF SHOCK OR FRIGHT HAD TO DO WITH THE FACT THAT SHE COULDN'T IMAGINE SETH HARMING ANYONE, LEAST OF ALL HER. AS HARD AS SHE TRIED, SHE WAS NEVER ABLE TO RECONCILE THE IDEA OF SETH KILLGORE, ALWAYS IN CONTROL, ALWAYS CALM WITH THE IMAGE SHE HAD IN HER MIND OF A BLOODTHIRSTY, MONSTROUS VAMPIRE.

EVEN THOUGH SHE FELT NO TRUE FEAR,

SHE REALIZED IT WAS PROBABLY FOR THE BEST THAT SHE STAY BEHIND THE LOCKED DOOR OF HER ROOM AS LONG AS SHE COULD. AT LEAST UNTIL CAIN GOT BACK.

BUT, HOURS LATER, WHEN NEITHER PETER NOR CAIN HAD RETURNED, CALLS OF NATURE MADE STAYING IN HER ROOM IMPOSSIBLE.

SLOWLY, AND WITH SOME HESITATION, SHE PADDED TOWARDS THE DOOR OF HER SMALL, BARE ROOM, UNLOCKED AND OPENED THE DOOR.

SHE'D BARELY STEPPED OUTSIDE WHEN SHE THE SIGHT OF SETH MADE HER STOP IN HER TRACKS.

HE WAS STANDING ACROSS FROM THE LONG COUCH, PACING A HOLE IN THE FLOOR. HIS HAIR WAS IN A GREATER STATE OF DISARRAY THAN SHE HAD EVER SEEN IT. THE EBONY LOCKS STUCK UP AT ALL ENDS WHEN SHE LOOKED AT HIS FACE, IT WAS MORE STARK AND PALE THAN IT HAD EVER BEEN BEFORE. HIS USUALLY BRIGHT PINK LIPS WERE NEARLY AS PALE AS HIS SKIN AND CHAPPED AT THE ENDS.

HE DIDN'T LOOK LIKE THE MAN SHE KNEW. IN FACT, IF SHE DIDN'T KNOW BETTER, SHE WOULD HAVE THOUGHT A STRANGER HAD BROKEN INTO THE HOUSE. EVEN WHEN SHE

RECOGNIZED SETH FOR WHO SHE WAS, SHE COULDN'T SEEM TO STOP HERSELF FROM STARING AT HIM.

MAYBE IT WAS INEVITABLE THEN THAT HE TURNED AND SAW HER.

WHEN HE DID, HIS EYES WIDENED AS THOUGH HE'D SEEN A GHOST. HIS PALE SKIN TURNED AN EVEN MORE GHOSTLY WHITE.

"ANDI!" HE SAID FIERCELY. "WHAT ARE YOU DOING? YOU SHOULDN'T BE OUT HERE."

"I'M NOT ALLOWED TO GO TO THE BATHROOM?" SHE ASKED.

HE LOOKED AT HER AS THOUGH HE WANTED TO SAY 'NO' AND ORDER HER BACK TO HER ROOM WHERE SHE WOULD BE FORCED TO HOLD HER BLADDER. FINALLY, THOUGH, HIS MIND SEEMED TO RELENT.

"JUST MAKE IT QUICK," HE SAID.

SHE MADE IT AS QUICK AS SHE POSSIBLY COULD. THOUGH, THERE WAS A BIT OF LINGERING OVER THE SINK AS SHE STARED AT HERSELF IN THE MIRROR. SHE REALIZED THAT THE SIGHT OF HER WAS NEARLY AS BAD AS SETH. HER SKIN, THOUGH NOT NEARLY AS WHITE AS HIS HAD GONE SLIGHTLY PALER. THE LONG, DIRTY BLONDE LOCKS OF HER HAIR,

93

USUALLY BRIGHT, BOBBY WAVES WERE NOW A MESS OF TANGLED FLY AWAY STRANDS.

WELL, SHE THOUGHT TO HERSELF, WHATEVER SELF-CONTROL SETH WAS AFRAID HE WOULDN'T BE ABLE TO MASTER, HER APPEARANCE WASN'T GOING TO MAKE IT ANY MORE DIFFICULT. SHE DIDN'T THINK A SEX STARVED MONK WOULD WANT HER TONIGHT. NOT THE WAY SHE LOOKED.

THAT WAS WHY HER HEART TURNED OVER IN SHOCK WHEN, AS SHE EXITED THE BATHROOM, SHE FOUND SETH AT THE DOOR, STARING AT HER WITH A HUNGRY EXPRESSION; AS THOUGH HE WANTED NOTHING MORE THAN TO TAKE HER IN HIS ARMS AND DEVOUR HER WHOLE.

"YOU'D-YOU'D BETTER GET BACK INSIDE," HE SAID. GREY EYES STILL LOCKED ON HERS. SHE NODDED BUT, HER LEGS DIDN'T SEEM TO WANT TO MOVE.

"I'LL...I'LL LOCK THE DOOR WHEN I GET IN IF YOU WANT ME TO."

"NOT A QUESTION OF WANTING," HE SAID. HIS VOICE HAD BECOME STRANGELY THICK. "BUT, YEAH. YOU SHOULD LOCK YOUR DOOR."

"I DON'T SUPPOSE YOU'LL TELL ME WHY," SHE SAID.

"YOU KNOW, DON'T YOU?" HE ASKED. "YOU WERE LISTENING TO ME AND CAIN AT THE DOOR."

"AND HERE I THOUGHT I'D BEEN QUIET THIS TIME," SHE SAID TRYING TO SMILE AND FAILING. HER HEART BEGAN TO POUND MORE QUICKLY AS HE TOOK A STEP TOWARDS HER. HIS GRAY EYES NEVER LEAVING HERS.

"ANDI...YOU'VE GOT TO GO. NOW," HE SAID. "IF YOU DON'T...I'LL BITE YOU. I KNOW I WILL. AND IF THAT HAPPENS."

ANDI NODDED AND THIS TIME FORCED HER LEGS TO MOVE. AS SOON AS THEY DID, HER FEET CAUGHT ON AN UNSEEN OBSTACLE IN THE MIDDLE OF THE FLOOR. SHE FELT HERSELF BEGIN TO FALL WHEN A QUICK, LONG, WARM ARM JUTTED OUT TO CATCH HER BY THE WAIST KEEPING HER UPRIGHT.

"PETER AND HIS DAMN SANDALS," SHE MUTTERED AT THE OFFENDING FOOTWEAR. "I KEEP TELLING HIM NOT TO-"

HER WORDS WERE STOPPED FULLY IN HER THROAT WHEN SHE TURNED AND CAME FACE TO FACE WITH SETH, HIS LIPS ONLY INCHES FROM HERS. THE DESPERATE, HUNGRY LOOK IN HIS EYES HAD INTENSIFIED BEYOND EXPRESSION. HIS ARM WAS STILL CIRCLED

AROUND HER WAIST, WARM AND SURE.

BETWEEN THE FEEL OF HIS SKIN THROUGH THE FABRIC OF HER NIGHTSHIRT AND HIS ODDLY WARM BREATH ON HER FACE, ANDI DECIDED THAT SHE COULDN'T STAND THIS ANYMORE. THE DANCING AROUND EACH OTHER, THE KISSING OF HANDS AND DESPERATELY WANTING MORE.

WITH A SMALL, FRUSTRATED SOUND IN THE BACK OF HER THROAT, SHE WRAPPED HER FREE ARM AROUND HIS NECK AND PULLED HIS LIPS DOWN TO MEET WITH HERS.

HE WAS WARMER THAN SHE EXPECTED, HIS LIPS AT FIRST SOFT AND THEN A THOUSAND TIMES MORE INTENSE AS HE BEGAN TO DEMAND ENTRANCE INTO HER MOUTH.

THOUGH SHE INITIATED THE KISS, HE QUICKLY TOOK CONTROL AFTER THAT, HIS OTHER ARM MOVED TO HER BACK AND PRESSED HER FIERCELY AGAINST HIS STRONG CHEST. THROUGH THE THIN SHIRT, HE WORE, SHE COULD FEEL HIS MUSCLES TIGHTEN AS HIS LIPS BECAME MUCH MORE INSISTENT.

THE DEEPER HE PUSHED HIS LIPS TO HERS, SHE FOUND HERSELF BEGINNING TO SEARCH FOR THE USUALLY HIDDEN FANGS, WONDERING, ALMOST ACADEMICALLY, HOW IT WOULD FEEL TO HAVE THEM PRESS INTO HER

SKIN.

ALL THOUGHTS WERE PUSHED ASIDE WHEN HIS STRONG ARMS LIFTED HER BODILY AND, IN A FRENZY, SHOVED HER UP AGAINST THE DOOR TO HER ROOM.

ANDI FELT THE PAIN OF THE COLLISION ONLY VAGUELY IN HER BACK. IT WAS REPLACED BY A SENSATION OF EUPHORIA WHEN SETH, STILL HOLDING HER WITH ONE HAND BY THE WAIST, SHOVED HIS LEG BETWEEN HER OWN WHILE HIS FREE HAND SNAKED ITS WAY DESPERATELY UP HER SHIRT. A GASP WAS RENTED FROM THE BOTTOM OF ANDI'S THROAT AS SETH CUPPED HER BREAST AND HIS LEG BEGAN TO MOVE AGAINST HER CENTER, STILL COVERED BY HER PAJAMA PANTS.

AT THE SOUND OF HER PLEASURABLE GASP, SETH MOVED HIS MOUTH FROM HERS WITH A GUTTURAL MOAN. AS THOUGH HE WAS A MAN DYING OF THIRST WHO WAS, AT LAST, BEING PRESENTED WITH A TALL, COOL DRINK OF WATER.

HIS LIPS MOVED BACK TO HER TRACING HER JAW AND THEN MOVING DOWN TO HER NECK, HIS TONGUE AND LIPS SUCKING NEAR THE HOLLOW OF HER THROAT.

ANDI LIFTED HER OWN HAND AND

TANGLED IT IN HIS LONG, DARK HAIR. IT WAS THAT MOVEMENT, FOR ONE REASON OR ANOTHER THAT GAVE HIM PAUSE, HIS LEG, THOUGH STILL BETWEEN HERS STOPPED MOVING. HIS HAND, THOUGH STILL INTENT ON CUPPING HER RIGHT BREAST, STILLED AS WELL. HE, APPARENTLY RELUCTANTLY, LIFTED HIS LIPS FROM HER NECK AND LOOKED INTO HER EYES.

"ANDI...I....WE SHOULDN'T," HE SAID. "I DON'T KNOW IF I'LL BE ABLE TO-"

"YOU WILL. I KNOW YOU WON'T HURT ME," ANDI SAID DESPERATELY. "I TRUST YOU."

"YOU SHOULDN'T," SETH SAID. HIS LEG MOVED FROM BETWEEN HERS NEARLY CAUSING A FRUSTRATED WHINE TO ESCAPE HER LIPS. HE BEGAN TO TAKE HIS HAND FROM BENEATH HER SHIRT AS WELL. FORCEFULLY, SHE GRABBED HIM BY THE WRIST AND MOVED HIS PALM AND FINGERS BACK UP TO CUP HER.

"YOU DON'T GET TO TELL ME WHAT I SHOULD AND SHOULDN'T DO," SHE TOLD HIM IN A HARSH WHISPER. SHE TOOK HER OTHER HAND AND PRESSED IT BETWEEN THEM TO HIS PROTRUDING AND VERY ERECT MEMBER. SETH GROANED.

"...OR WHAT I SHOULD OR SHOULDN'T WANT."

"ANDI," HE SAID, HIS VOICE GROWLING, HALF WITH LUST AND HALF WITH A WARNING.

"AND I WANT YOU," SHE WHISPERED TO HIM. HER HAND BEGAN TO MOVE UP AND DOWN HIS STILL CLOTHED SHAFT. "I'VE WANTED YOU FOR A LONG TIME. I KNOW YOU HAVE TOO. SO, WHAT ARE YOU WAITING FOR?"

THAT, APPARENTLY, WAS ALL THE ENCOURAGEMENT HE NEEDED. HIS LEG RESUMED ITS MOVEMENT, CAUSING SHIVERS OF ECSTASY TO MOVE UP AND DOWN HER SPINE. HIS HAND MOVED FROM UNDERNEATH HER SHIRT AND TURNED THE KNOB ON THE DOOR.

JUST AS SHE FELT SHE WAS ABOUT TO FALL THROUGH IT, HE LIFTED HER, ONCE AGAIN, BODILY FROM THE FLOOR AND, HIS MOUTH RETURNING FERVENTLY TO HERS, BEGAN TO CARRY HER TO THE BED.

THOUGH HIS HANDS WERE SURE AND HIS HOLD MORE THAN STRONG, EVEN THEN AS HE DROPPED HER ONTO THE COVERS OF THE SMALL BED IN HER ROOM, SHE FELT AS THOUGH HE WAS HOLDING BACK FROM HER. AS THOUGH HE WAS NOT TRULY THERE, WITH HER.

WHEN SHE LOOKED INTO HIS EYES AS HE

CLIMBED ON TOP OF HER, HIS HANDS ROAMING HER STILL CLOTHED FORM, SHE SAW THIS HINT OF RESERVATION CONFIRMED.

SHE GASPED AGAIN IN PROTEST. WHEN HE TOOK HIS HANDS OFF HER SIDE. BUT, WHEN SHE LOOKED INTO HIS EYES, SHE WAS MET WITH A LOOK TWICE AS INTENSE AND A MILLION TIMES AS INTIMATE AS ANY TOUCH HE COULD POSSIBLY HAVE GIVEN HER.

"DON'T LET ME BITE YOU," HE WHISPERED FINALLY.

THE EXPRESSION IN HIS EYES, MORE SERIOUS THAN SHE'D THOUGHT POSSIBLE TOLD HER THAT HE MEANT THIS, ABSOLUTELY.

"OK," SHE SAID WITH A NOD. A LOOK OF RELIEF PASSED OVER HIS FACE, HIS HANDS RETURNED TO HER SHIRT BUT THE RESERVATION WAS STILL THERE. SHE KNEW JUST WHAT TO DO ABOUT THAT.

"I JUST HOPE YOU DON'T MIND IF...I BITE YOU."

A WICKED GRIN SPREAD ACROSS HER FACE AS SHE MOVED HER HANDS UP HIS PALE TORSO, LIFTED HIS SHIRT AND MOVED HER MOUTH TO KISS THE SMOOTH, COOL, TAUGHT SKIN.

"MMM," HE GROANED IN SATISFACTION AS

HE ALLOWED HER TO PULL THE SHIRT UP AND OVER HIS HEAD WHILE HER LIPS CONTINUED TO MOVE LOWER.

SOON, SHE'D RELIEVED HIM OF HIS PANTS AND HE, IN TURN, HAD PUSHED HER SHIRT UP AND OFF OF HER BODY, REVEALING HER LARGE BREASTS.

HER MOUTH LICKED AND NIPPED ALONG HIS INNER THIGH CAUSING A SERIES OF MUTTERED CURSES AND GROANS. A FIRM HAND GRABBED HER HAIR TRYING TO FORCE HER UP WHERE HE NEEDED HER TO BE. ENJOYING THIS TEASING GAME TOO MUCH, SHE SMILED AT HIM AND RETURNED TO HER WORK, LIPS BARELY BRUSHING HIS ERECT AND LEAKING MEMBER.

THIS WAS TOO MUCH FOR HIM. AND, WITH A FRUSTRATED GROWL, HE PULLED AT HER HAIR, FORCING HER FROM HER POSITION. ONCE SHE WAS UP, HE GRABBED HER SHOULDERS AND PINNED HER DOWN ON THE BED.

"SO YOU LIKE TO TEASE, HUH?" HE ASKED. "YOU LIKE TO PLAY GAMES?"

"GAMES CAN BE FUN," SHE SAID, LIFTING HER STILL CLOTHED HIPS TO RUB AGAINST HIS MEMBER. "YOU SHOULD TRY THEM SOMETIME."

HE PUSHED HIS LEGS FORCIBLY AGAINST

HER HIPS WHICH IMMEDIATELY HALTED THEIR MOVEMENT.

"I DON'T PLAY GAMES," HE WHISPERED. ONE OF HIS HANDS FOUND ITS WAY BETWEEN HER LEGS AND PRESSED FIRMLY AGAINST HER CENTER. SHE LET OUT A SMALL NOISE, WHETHER IT WAS ONE OF PAIN OR ONE OF PLEASURE, SHE COULDN'T BE ENTIRELY SURE.

"I WANT YOU," HE SAID. "AND I'LL TAKE YOU."

A STRONG SHIVER RUSHED DOWN HER SPINE AS HE PULLED HER SLEEP PANTS DOWN AND, IN ONE MOVE, THRUST INSIDE OF HER.

THE GROAN HE EMITTED, UNCONTROLLED AND UNRESERVED, WAS SUCH A DEPARTURE FROM WHAT SHE KNEW OF HIM, THAT SHE COULD DO LITTLE NOW BUT WATCH AS HE PUSHED AGAINST HER SHOULDERS, THRUSTING HIMSELF INSIDE OF HER AGAIN AND AGAIN. TAKING EXACTLY WHAT HE HAD PROMISED HE WOULD.

SHE WRAPPED HER ARMS AROUND HIS NECK, MEETING HIM, AS BEST SHE COULD, THRUST FOR THRUST UNTIL, FINALLY HER CRY MINGLED WITH HIS AND BOTH BOUNCED OFF THE WALLS OF THE TINY, BARE ROOM.

THEY STAYED LIKE THAT FOR A LONG

WHILE AFTERWARD. WRAPPED TOGETHER, SWEAT AND TEARS AND LIMBS MIXING AND MINGLING. EVENTUALLY, HE ROLLED OFF OF HER AND SHE TURNED TO LOOK AT HIM.

HIS FACE WAS STILL PALER THAN SHE WOULD HAVE LIKED BUT NOW A LITTLE FLUSHED FROM THE EXERCISE. HE MET HER EYES ONLY BRIEFLY, THEN LOOKED DOWN AT HIS NAVEL WITH AN APOLOGETIC GLANCE AS THOUGH HALF ASHAMED OF WHAT HE...WHAT THEY HAD JUST DONE.

"DON'T YOU DARE SAY YOU'RE SORRY," ANDI SAID CUTTING OFF THE APOLOGY SHE FEARED AT THE START. "WE'VE BOTH WANTED THAT FOR WEEKS AND YOU CAN'T PRETEND LIKE WE DIDN'T."

"I WASN'T GOING TO SAY SORRY," SETH TOLD HER FINALLY. "AND, YOU'RE RIGHT. TRUTH IS, I'VE WANTED THAT SINCE THE FIRST TIME I SAW YOU."

HE GLANCED UP AT HER, A GENUINE HALF SMILE ON HIS FACE. THE KIND THAT MADE HIS EYES DANCE.
"WELL THEN," SHE SAID. "ENJOY IT."

WITHOUT WAITING FOR HIS PERMISSION, SHE ROLLED INTO HIM AND PULLED HIS ARMS TIGHT AROUND HER. HE KEPT THEM THERE AND SEEMED TO SETTLE INTO HER

COMFORTABLY.

"I WILL," HE PROMISED. "THOUGH, REALLY, WE WEREN'T SUPPOSED TO DO THAT UNTIL THE MATING."

"SO, THAT'S WHAT THE MATING IS?" SHE ASKED. "YOU COULD'VE TOLD ME THAT WEEKS AGO. DIDN'T HAVE TO BE A BIG MYSTERY."

"THAT'S ONLY HALF OF IT," HE SAID. "WHAT'S THE OTHER HALF?"

HE SIGHED INTO HER HAIR AND SHE FELT HIS ARMS TENSE JUST SLIGHTLY.

"LOOK," SHE SAID HALF IRRITABLE, THOUGH SHE STAYED NESTLED IN HIS ARMS, HER BACK TO HIM. "WE'VE ALREADY DONE HALF OF IT. YOU MIGHT AS WELL TELL ME THE REST."

"I GUESS I SHOULD," SETH SAID WITH A SIGH. STILL, HE HESITATED BEFORE SPEAKING AGAIN.

"I HAVE TO DRINK YOUR BLOOD," HE SAID FINALLY. THIS CAUSED HER TO TURN IN HIS ARMS WITH A CONFUSED FROWN.

"BUT...I THOUGHT YOU WEREN'T SUPPOSED TO BITE ME," SHE SAID.

"I WON'T," HE ANSWERED. "YOU HAVE TO GIVE ME A LITTLE BIT OF YOUR BLOOD, FREELY. AND THEN, I GIVE YOU A BIT OF MINE. AGAIN, FREELY."

"OH," WAS ALL SHE COULD SAY. SHE TURNED AROUND AGAIN IN HIS ARMS, HER BACK FACING HIM.

"AND...WE CAN'T DO THAT 'TILL WE GET TO NEW YORK?"

"WELL, TECHNICALLY, WE COULD DO IT RIGHT HERE," HE SAID. "WE DON'T NEED WITNESSES OR AN OFFICIANT FOR A MATING. BUT, MY PARENTS WANT TO BE THERE FOR THE MATING. AND IT'S ALWAYS BEEN DONE ON A FULL MOON IN THE PRESENCE OF THE CLAN BEFORE. DON'T WANT TO BREAK TRADITION."

"I SEE," SHE SAID. "AND...WHEN WE'RE MATED...THESE THINGS CAN'T HURT ME, RIGHT?"

"IF THEY TRY TO KILL YOU IT WILL STRIP THEM OF THEIR POWER," HE SAID. "ESSENTIALLY THEY'LL DIE. THAT'S WHY THEY'RE AFTER YOU NOW."

A SMILE CREPT BACK ONTO HER FACE AS SHE TURNED BACK TO FACE HIM.

"THAT'S WHY I'M GLAD YOU'RE HERE TO

PROTECT ME," SHE SAID SWEETLY. HE LET OUT A SMALL CHUCKLE AND WRAPPED HIS ARMS MORE FIRMLY AROUND HER.

"SOMETHING TELLS ME YOU DON'T REALLY NEED ME TO PROTECT YOU," HE SAID. SHE WAS ABOUT TO TELL HIM HOW TRUE THAT WAS WHEN THE CHUCKLE IN HIS VOICE TURNED INTO A DEEP AND WORRYING COUGH.

"YOU OK?" SHE ASKED.

"FINE," HE SAID. "I JUST NEED...FOOD."

"YOU MEAN BLOOD?"

HE NODDED BUT SEEMED UNABLE TO SAY THE WORD.

"CAIN SHOULD BE BACK ANY MINUTE WITH IT," HE SAID.

"WELL. YOU SHOULD REST UNTIL HE COMES," SHE ANSWERED MOVING HERSELF TO A COMFORTABLE POSITION INSIDE HIS EMBRACE.

HE DIDN'T PROTEST AND IT WASN'T LONG BEFORE ANDI HEARD HIM SNORING BEHIND HER. AND, NOT LONG AFTER THAT, SHE CLOSED HER EYES AND WELCOMED OBLIVION AS WELL.

WHAT SEEMED LIKE ONLY MOMENTS LATER, SHE WAS JOLTED AWAKE BY A FIRM AND VERY COLD HAND COVERING HER MOUTH. AT FIRST, SHE THOUGHT IT HAD COME FROM SETH UNTIL SHE LOOKED OVER TO THE OTHER SIDE OF THE BED AND FOUND HIM STILL LYING FAST ASLEEP.

SHE LIFTED HER EYES AND SAW A DARK HOODED FIGURE. SHE OPENED HER MOUTH TO SCREAM BUT BEFORE SHE COULD, AN EXTREMELY FAMILIAR VOICE ISSUED FROM THE STRANGE FIGURE'S DIRECTION.

"TRY ANYTHING," HE SAID. "AND YOU BOTH

DIE."

Chapter Six

CAIN, ONE HAND STILL CLASPED OVER
ANDI'S MOUTH, GRABBED HER ARM AND
PULLED HER FORCEFULLY FROM THE BED.
ANDI STILLED HER FEET AND WRESTLED AS
BEST SHE COULD BUT IT WAS NO USE. HIS HOLD
WAS STRONGER THAN ANY OTHER MAN SHE
HAD EVER MET, INCLUDING SETH.

WHEN HE PUSHED THE ONLY HALF CLOSED
DOOR TO THE ROOM OPEN, HER EYES BLINKED
AGAINST THE SUDDENLY BRIGHT LIGHTS IN
THE OUTER LIVING SPACE.

ONCE HER SLEEP FILLED EYES HAD
ADJUSTED, SHE COULDN'T HELP THE SCREAM
THAT TORE OUT OF HER THROAT.
PETER WAS LYING ON THE COUCH, EYES
CLOSED AND UNRESPONSIVE. HIS BACK FACING
THEM.

FLANKED ON EITHER SIDE OF HIM WERE
TWO MEN...NO...NOT MEN...CREATURES IN
BLACK, FLOWING ROBES, WITH RED EYES AND
SKIN SO WHITE THAT ANDI COULD SEE EACH
VEIN THROBBING INSIDE THEIR BALD SKULLS.
THEIR MOUTHS, IF YOU COULD CALL THEM
THAT, WERE NO MORE THAN LIPLESS SLITS
WHERE TWO LARGE FANGS PROTRUDED AND

AT THE END OF THEIR WRINKLED AND
GNARLED HANDS, THE BLACK, CLAW LIKE
NAILS WHICH HAD GRASPED HER THE FIRST
NIGHT IN THAT CLUB.

CAIN LED HER TO THESE CREATURES,
THOUGH SHE STRUGGLED VIOLENTLY
AGAINST THE PROSPECT OF BEING ANYWHERE
NEAR THEM. IT WASN'T UNTIL HE FORCED HER
ONTO THE COUCH, RIGHT NEXT TO PETER'S
LIMP BACK LEGS, THAT HE TOOK HIS HAND
AWAY FROM HER MOUTH.

BUT NOT BEFORE HE BENT DOWN AND
WHISPERED.

"YOU SCREAM, YOU SAY A WORD, YOU SO
MUCH AS MUTTER, I SWEAR I'LL LEAVE YOU TO
THE MERCY OF MY FRIENDS," HE SAID. "AND I
PROMISE THEY'RE NOT AS NICE AS I AM."

GLANCING ON EITHER SIDE OF HER ARE
CAIN TOOK HIS HAND AWAY AND MOVED TO
THE BACK OF THE COUCH, ANDI DECIDED IT
WAS BEST, FOR THE TIME BEING, TO DO AS SHE
WAS TOLD. THOUGH SHE THOUGHT RUEFULLY,
SHE HAD NEVER BEEN MUCH GOOD AT
KEEPING HER MOUTH SHUT.

"NOW," CAIN SAID. "ONCE WE'VE GOT YOU
FIRMLY TIED, WE'LL GO AND GET SETH."

HE MOVED BACK TO HER AND, SITTING

BEHIND HER, JUST NEXT TO PETER'S TORSO, HE FORCED HER BACK TO HIM AND PULLED HER HANDS BEHIND HER. SHE FELT HER WRIST BEING PUSHED TOGETHER AND TIED TIGHTLY WITH A ROPE.

"WHAT ARE YOU DOING?" SHE ASKED QUIETLY, STRAINING HER NECK SO THAT SHE COULD SEE HIM BEHIND HER.

HE LOOKED UP AT HER, DARK EYES GLARING IN AN EXPRESSION SHE HAD NEVER SEEN FROM HIM.

"I TOLD YOU NOT TO SPEAK," HE SAID. FOR A MOMENT, SHE WAS FRIGHTENED. TRULY FRIGHTENED THAT HE JUST MIGHT LET THOSE HORRIBLE CREATURES, THE STRIGA, SHE SUPPOSED, LOOSE ON HER. A MOMENT LATER, HOWEVER, HIS FACE SOFTENED.

"STILL," HE SAID STILL TYING THE ROPE TIGHTLY AROUND HER WRISTS. "I GUESS I OWE YOU AN EXPLANATION. YOU SEE, SETH NEEDS BLOOD. YOU MAY HAVE NOTICED THAT I'VE BEEN SLOWLY DEPLETING THE SUPPLY HE BROUGHT ALONG. THOUGH, YOU PROBABLY DIDN'T. I ONLY TOOK TWO VIALS A DAY TO THROW OUT. I KNEW HE WOULDN'T REALIZE THAT THEY'D GONE MISSING. BUT, AS A RESULT, HE HASN'T EATEN IN...TWO DAYS NOW. AND, I'M SURE HE'S STARVING."

HE FINISHED HIS KNOT. IT WAS TIGHT ENOUGH THAT ANDI FELT THE ROPES CUTTING INTO HER WRISTS.

"SO," CAIN CONTINUED, LOOKING UP AT HER. "I THOUGHT HE MIGHT ENJOY DRINKING YOURS."

HER EYES WIDENED AND SHE WRINKLED HER BROW IN CONFUSION. HALF OF HER WANTED TO SPIT IN CAIN'S FACE IN DEFIANCE. HALF OF HER WANTED TO KNEE HIM IN THE BALLS AND RUN. IN FACT, IF IT HADN'T BEEN FOR THE SILENT BUT TERRIFYING PRESENCE OF THE STRIGA TO HER RIGHT AND LEFT, SHE WOULDN'T HAVE HESITATED TO DO THE LATTER.

BUT, AT THE MOMENT, THE ONLY THING SHE COULD FORCE OUT OF HER MOUTH WAS.

"WHY THE HELL WOULD YOU DO THIS? HE'S YOUR BROTHER."

A DARK CLOUD FLEW SUDDENLY OVER CAIN'S FACE. HIS EYES NARROWED AT ANDI AND, FOR THE FIRST TIME SINCE THEY'D MET, SHE FELT A TWINGE OF FEAR WHEN SHE LOOKED AT HIM.

"HE IS NOT MY BROTHER," CAIN SNARLED. "HE'S NOTHING MORE THAN SOME MORTAL MY MOTHER AND FATHER PICKED OUT OF A

FOREST. MY MOTHER STUPIDLY NAMED HIM SUCCESSOR BEFORE I WAS BORN. WELL, I GUESS THAT WAS UNDERSTANDABLE. SHE DIDN'T THINK SHE WOULD BE ABLE TO PRODUCE A DYMPHIRE. BUT, WHEN I CAME ALONG, SHE REFUSED TO TAKE IT BACK! SHE REFUSED TO NAME ME AS THE SUCCESSOR INSTEAD! NOW, I DON'T HAVE A CHOICE. I HAVE TO CLAIM MY BIRTHRIGHT."

"BY WORKING WITH THESE...THESE THINGS?" ANDI ASKED. SHE TOOK A CHANCE TO GLARE AS STRONGLY AS SHE COULD AT THE CREATURE TO HER RIGHT. ALL THE COURAGE LEFT HER WHEN ITS RED EYES MOVED BACK TO HER, GLOWING RED.

"THESE THINGS AS YOU CALL THEM," CAIN SAID. "ARE STRONGER THAN MY BROTHER OR MY FATHER WILL EVER BE. THEY KNOW THE WAY OF THE WORLD. THE STRONG SURVIVE AND THAT'S ALL THERE IS TO IT. IF HUMANITY IS NOT STRONG ENOUGH TO DEFEAT THE STRIGA, IT DOESN'T DESERVE TO CONTINUE." ANOTHER FIERCE URGE TO SPIT AT HIM, KICK HIM, CALL HIM EVERY FOUL NAME SHE COULD THINK OF FILLED ANDI'S HEART. BUT, THERE WAS MORE TO THINK ABOUT NOW THAN HER RIGHTEOUS INDIGNATION. SHE GLANCED BESIDE HER ON THE COUCH AT THE FORM OF HER COUSIN, SPLAYED OUT.

"WHAT'VE YOU DONE TO PETER?" SHE

113

ASKED.

"DON'T WORRY," CAIN SAID. "HE'S NOT DEAD. WE USED THE SAME DRUG ON HIM THAT WE USED ON YOU THAT NIGHT AT THE CLUB. WHEN HE WAKES UP, THIS WILL ALL BE OVER."

ANDI FELT HER HEART GIVE A SMALL LEAP OF RELIEF. THAT, AT THE VERY LEAST, WAS SOMETHING. NOT MUCH OF SOMETHING IF, WHEN PETER WOKE UP, SHE AND SETH WERE BOTH DEAD. BUT, IT WAS SOMETHING NONE THE LESS.

AND SHE ALLOWED THAT SOMETHING TO GROW INSIDE HER, A SMALL LIGHT OF HOPE WHEN CAIN SPOKE NEXT.
"NOW, I THINK WE'LL BRING SETH OUT TO PLAY," HE SAID. AND, WITH A CUNNING SMILE, HE STOOD FROM THE PLACE WHERE HE SAT AND MOVED INTO THE NEXT ROOM.

WHEN HE CLOSED THE DOOR BEHIND HIM, ANDI TRIED TO THINK OF SOMETHING ANYTHING THAT MIGHT GET HER, THEM, OUT OF THIS.

THAT WAS WHEN SHE REMEMBERED. PETER CARRIED A SMALL POCKET KNIFE IN THE BACK OF HIS JEANS. AND, IF SHE REMEMBERED CORRECTLY, IT WAS IN THE POCKET CURRENTLY LODGED JUST BEHIND HER.

HER HANDS, TIED BEHIND HER, FELT ALONG PETER'S BACK POCKETS. TRYING TO IGNORE THE THOUGHT THAT SHE WAS CURRENTLY FRISKING HER COUSIN'S BUTT. SHE REMINDED HERSELF IT WAS FOR A VERY GOOD CAUSE.

AFTER ONLY A MOMENT'S SEARCH, SHE REVEALED THAT IT WAS, INDEED THERE. NOW, ALL SHE HAD TO DO WAS GET IT TO THE TOP, WHERE SHE COULD GRAB HOLD OF IT.

"IN HERE," CAIN WAS SAYING. "I GOT AS MUCH BLOOD AS I COULD."

THE DOOR HAD JUST OPENED AND SHE COULD SEE CAIN'S OUTLINE STEPPING OUT OF THE DOOR AND HOLDING IT OPEN.

"YOU STILL HAVEN'T TOLD ME WHERE ANDI-"

SETH'S VOICE STOPPED DEAD AND HIS EYES GREW WIDE WHEN HE LOOKED FROM ANDI TO PETE BEHIND HER AND FINALLY TO THE STRIGA ON EITHER SIDE OF THEM.

"YOU NEED BLOOD," CAIN SAID WITH A MALEVOLENT SMILE. "HERE IT IS."

HE MADE A GRAND GESTURE TO ANDI WRIGGLING ON THE COUCH AS THOUGH IN A VAIN ATTEMPT TO GET FREE. IN REALITY, SHE

HAD NEARLY FREED HER COUSIN'S KNIFE FROM THE CONFINES OF ITS POCKET. "YOU-" SETH BEGAN, HIS FACE FLITTING BETWEEN CONFUSION, HORROR, AND FURY.

"YOU DIDN'T THINK I HAD IT IN ME, DID YOU, SETH?" CAIN ASKED IN THE SAME MALEVOLENT TONE. "DIDN'T THINK I WOULD DARE TO QUESTION MOM AND DAD WHEN THEY NAMED YOU SUCCESSOR. DIDN'T THINK I WOULD TRY TO CLAIM MY BIRTH RIGHT?"

"CAIN, IT'S NOT A BIRTHRIGHT!" SETH SAID FURIOUSLY TO HIS BROTHER EVEN WHILE HIS GRAY EYES REMAINED WIDE AND FIXED ON ANDI. "IT'S A-"

"A RESPONSIBILITY," CAIN SPAT BACK. "YEAH, I'VE HEARD MOM SAY THAT TOO. I'VE HEARD HER SAY THAT I'M NOT RESPONSIBLE ENOUGH. I'M TOO WEAK TO HANDLE IT. WELL, NOW I'M GOING TO PROVE HER WRONG."

"IT'S NOT ABOUT BEING WEAK, CAIN," SETH SAID. "YOU DON'T KNOW WHAT YOU'RE-"

"OH, I KNOW EXACTLY WHAT I'M DOING, BROTHER," HE SAID. "AND, RIGHT NOW, YOU'RE THE ONE WHO LOOKS A BIT WEAK."

ANDI EYED SETH WHO WAS, INDEED, LOOKING THIN. HIS HANDS SHAKING. THE MOMENT SHE TOOK NOTE OF THAT, SHE FELT

THE KNIFE IN PETER'S POCKET FINALLY POKE OUT. SHE BEGAN TO MOVE HER HANDS SUBTLY UP AND DOWN, CUTTING THE KNOT IN THE ROPE.

"GO ON, SETH," CAIN SAID. "DRINK FROM HER."

AS ANDI CONTINUED TO MOVE UP AND DOWN FREEING HER HANDS FROM THE ROPE, SHE SAW THE LITTLE BLOOD LEFT IN SETH'S FACE DRAIN OUT OF IT.

"NO," HE SAID FIERCELY SHAKING HIS HEAD. "YOU KNOW I WON'T."

"I THOUGHT SO," CAIN SAID.

HE TURNED TO THE CREATURE TO ANDI'S LEFT AND SAID SOMETHING UNINTELLIGIBLE. SUDDENLY, THE CREATURE LITERALLY FLEW TO ANDI, ITS HAND GRASPING AT HER THROAT. ANDI GAVE A HIGH PITCHED GASP AS SHE MOVED UP AGAINST THE KNIFE, AT LAST, SECRETLY FREED HER HANDS FROM THE ROPES. THOUGH, WITH A STRIGA CLAW, CLASPED AROUND HER THROAT THAT WAS LITTLE COMFORT.

"YOU DRINK FROM HER," CAIN SAID. "OR THEY WILL. AND YOU KNOW BETTER THAN ANYONE. IF THEY DRINK FROM HER, SHE WON'T SURVIVE."

ANDI'S EYES GLANCED UP TO THE CREATURE ABOVE HER. AS SOON AS SHE DID, A FOUL STENCH LIKE ROTTING EGGS FLEW INTO HER NOSTRILS AS THE CREATURE OPENED ITS MOUTH REVEALING HIS LONG FANGS.

"GO ON," CAIN SAID. "SAVE HER. DRINK FROM HER AND SAVE HER."
THE TORMENT ON SETH'S FACE WAS SO PALPABLE THAT ANDI COULD FEEL IT TWISTING HER HEART IN TWO. HE STARED INTO HER EYES, SILENTLY BEGGING HER FORGIVENESS. SHE COULD TELL HE WANTED HER TO FORGIVE HIM FOR CHOOSING HER, FOR WANTING HER, FOR ALLOWING THIS TO HAPPEN IN THE FIRST PLACE.

HELPLESSLY, SHE STARED BACK WISHING THERE WAS SOMETHING SHE COULD DO.

THAT'S WHEN IT HIT HER. THERE WAS SOMETHING SHE COULD DO. THE KNIFE WAS STILL EXPOSED BEHIND HER. AWARE OF THE PUTRID CREATURE'S STILL FIRM HOLD ON HER THROAT, SHE SQUIRMED BACKWARD, HITTING THE EDGE OF HER WRIST AGAINST THE STILL UNSEEN KNIFE. SHE PRESSED BACK BITING HER LIP TO KEEP FROM CALLING OUT AS SHE FELT THE SKIN BREAK.

'THEY CAN'T HURT YOU IF YOU'RE ONE OF US.' THAT'S WHAT SETH HAD TOLD HER. SHE

HAD TO JOIN HIM IF EITHER OF THEM WERE GOING TO MAKE IT OUT OF THIS.

"THIS IS YOUR LAST CHANCE," CAIN WAS SAYING WITH AN EDGE OF IMPATIENCE TO HIS BROTHER. "EITHER TAKE HER NOW OR-"

"IT'S OK, SETH," SHE SAID. "JUST DRINK. TRUST ME. IT'LL BE FINE."

SETH'S EYES WENT SO WIDE THAT HIS DARK EYEBROWS RECEDED ALMOST COMPLETELY INTO HIS HAIRLINE.

"ANDI, YOU KNOW I WOULD NEVER-"

"SETH, PLEASE!" SHE SAID. "TRUST ME."

HER GREEN EYES NARROWED AT HIM AND SHE PRAYED WITH ALL HER MIGHT THAT HE WOULD UNDERSTAND THE SIGNIFICANT LOOK SHE WAS GIVING HIM. APPARENTLY, HE DID.

SLOWLY, HE MOVED AWAY FROM CAIN TOWARDS ANDI. SHE CAUGHT CAIN'S TRIUMPHANT SMILE A MOMENT BEFORE HE SAID SOMETHING UNINTELLIGIBLE IN WHAT SOUNDED LIKE ROMANIAN. IMMEDIATELY, THE STRIGA'S CLAWED GRIP LET GO OF HER THROAT AND GLIDED BACK TO ITS PLACE TO HER LEFT.

CAIN MOVED TO HER AND KNELT DOWN

119

BEFORE HER, LIKE A KNIGHT OF OLD PRESENTING A DRAGON TO HIS MAIDEN.

"WHAT ARE YOU DOING?" HE WHISPERED.

"HERE," SHE SAID CAREFULLY MOVING HER UNTIED AND CUT HAND OUT TO HIM, MAKING SURE THAT SETH'S BODY WAS COVERING THE MOTION THAT CAIN COULD NOT SEE. "DRINK FROM HERE. I'M GIVING IT TO YOU FREELY. UNDERSTAND?"

SHE NARROWED HER EYES AT HIM ONCE MORE IN A SIGNIFICANT EXPRESSION. HE NODDED IN UNDERSTANDING AND DIPPED HIS HEAD TO HER WRIST, DRINKING THE BLOOD EXPOSED. AS SOON AS HE DID, ANDI SAW A HINT OF LIFE RETURN TO HIS CHEEKS. HE, IN TURN, MOVED HIS OWN WRIST TO HIS LIPS.

"NOW YOU'LL DRINK FROM ME," HE SAID SOFTLY. WITH HIS FANGS, HE TORE A SLIT IN ONE WRIST. AS SOON AS HE DID, THE STRIGA TO THEIR RIGHT LET OUT AN UNEARTHLY SOUND. LIKE THE ONE SHE HAD HEARD THAT FIRST NIGHT AT THE CLUB.

IT GLIDED INCREDIBLY FAST TOWARD SETH TRYING TO SHOVE HIM TO THE GROUND. SETH STRUGGLED AGAINST THE CLAW LIKE HOLD ON HIS SHOULDERS HOLDING HIS WRIST OUT TO ANDI.

"ANDI!" HE CALLED AS SHE SHOT UP FROM THE SOFA. "DRINK NOW!"

SHE GRABBED HOLD OF SETH'S WRIST. THE MOMENT SHE DID, THE OTHER STRIGA'S CRY FILLED HER EARS AS IT GRABBED HER SHOULDERS AS WELL.

"STOP THEM!" CAIN WAS CRYING, SOUNDING, FOR THE FIRST TIME, TRULY FRIGHTENED, INSECURE.

IT TOOK ALL THE STRENGTH ANDI HAD INSIDE OF HER TO PULL AGAINST THE STRIGA'S HOLD AND KEEP HOLD OF SETH'S WRIST WHEN THE OTHER WAS PULLING HIM AWAY. FINALLY, SHE BROUGHT THE BRIGHT, RED BLOOD ON HIS WRIST CLOSE ENOUGH TO TOUCH HERS. STEELING HERSELF, SHE ALLOWED HER MOUTH TO COVER THE WOUND AND DRANK THE BLOOD THERE.

NO SOONER HAD THE METALLIC TASTE FILLED HER MOUTH THAN TWO UNEARTHLY SOUNDS FILLED HER EARS. AS SUDDENLY AS THE CLAWS HAD GRABBED HER SHOULDERS, THEY LET GO CAUSING HER TO FALL BACK AND CRASH ONTO THE COUCH.

"WHAT ARE YOU DOING? NO! NO! NOT ME, THEM! THEM!"

CAIN'S VOICE WAS CRYING OUT AGAINST

ANDI'S CLOSED EYES. WHEN SHE OPENED THEM, SHE SAW THE HORRIBLE STRIGA GRASPING AS HARD AS THEY COULD AT CAIN.

APPARENTLY, DEPRIVED OF THEIR PROMISED HUMAN MEAL, THEY WERE WILLING TO SETTLE FOR A DYMPHIRE.
SETH CRAWLED TOWARDS ANDI ON THE FLOOR AND PUT HER ARMS AROUND HER SHOULDERS AS SHE WATCHED IN HORROR AS ONE STRIGA HELD ONTO THE BACK OF A STRUGGLING CAIN WHILE THE OTHER OPENED ITS LARGE, MALFORMED MOUTH.

THE SMELL OF ROTTING EGGS AND SMOKE FILLED THE ROOM AS THE STRIGA'S LONG FANGS HIT AGAINST THE SIDE OF CAIN'S NECK. ANDI AND SETH WATCHED IN HORROR AS THE CREATURES FED. CAIN'S CRIES GROWING WEAKER AND WEAKER UNTIL FINALLY, THEY STOPPED ALTOGETHER AND HE FELL TO THE FLOOR IN A LIFELESS HEAP.
THE STRIGA DID NOT EVEN BOTHER TO LOOK BEHIND THEM AS THEY CLOSED THEIR WELL-FED MOUTHS NOW STREWN WITH BLOOD AND GLIDED TOWARDS THE LONE WINDOW IN THE BARE HOUSE. ANDI STARED AS THE TWO CREATURES MOVED THROUGH THE WALL AS THOUGH IT WERE NOTHING AND OUT INTO THE STILL DARK NIGHT.
SETH AND ANDI STAYED ON THE FLOOR, SETH'S ARM WRAPPED AROUND HER SHOULDER FOR WHAT SEEMED LIKE HOURS.

FINALLY, HE SHIFTED AND LOOKED AT HER.

"ARE YOU OK?" HE ASKED.

"ABOUT AS OK AS I COULD BE, CONSIDERING," SHE ANSWERED. "HOW ABOUT YOU?"

"I'LL BE FINE," HE SAID.

HIS GRAY EYES LOOKED INTO HERS AS THOUGH HE WANTED TO SAY SOMETHING ELSE BUT COULDN'T QUITE FORCE IT OUT. INSTEAD, HE LOOKED OVER HER SHOULDER TO PETER STILL LYING SPLAYED ON THE COUCH.

"WHAT ABOUT PETE?" HE ASKED.

ANDI, WITH SOME DIFFICULTY, STOOD UP AND MOVED TO HER COUSIN. SHE CHECKED HIS PULSE AND, SURE ENOUGH, THE BEAT WAS AS NORMAL AS COULD BE EXPECTED.

"HE'S ALIVE," SHE SAID. "CAIN SAID THEY USED THE SAME DRUG ON HIM THAT THEY USED ON ME IN THE CLUB. IF THAT'S THE CASE, HE'LL HAVE QUITE THE HEADACHE IN THE MORNING. BUT, HE SHOULD BE FINE."

SETH NODDED AND TURNED HIS EYES FROM HER TO CAIN. WHEN HE LOOKED AT HIS

BROTHER, PALE BODY DRAINED OF BLOOD
AND LIFE, HE SEEMED UNABLE TO MOVE,
UNABLE TO DO MUCH OF ANYTHING.

ANDI'S HEART GREW HEAVY IN HER CHEST
AT HIS EXPRESSION. NO MATTER WHAT CAIN
HAD DONE. NO MATTER HOW DEEPLY HE'D
BETRAYED THEM, HE HAD STILL BEEN SETH'S
BROTHER.

"HEY," ANDI SAID MOVING TO SETH AND
TAKING HIS HAND. "I'VE GOT TO CLEAN UP
THE CUT ON MY WRIST. THERE'RE BAND-AIDS
IN THE ROOM."

SHE TOOK HIS ARM AND LIFTED IT. HE
DIDN'T MOVE FOR A MOMENT. FOR A MOMENT,
SHE FEARED HE MIGHT NOT MOVE AGAIN. THE
MOMENT PASSED, HOWEVER, AND, A SECOND
LATER, HE LOOKED UP AT HER AND NODDED.

SHE LIFTED HIM FROM THE FLOOR AND
THEY MOVED INTO THE BEDROOM. SOON, HE
WAS CAREFULLY CLEANING THE RELATIVELY
SMALL CUT ON HER WRIST WITH A SWAB OF
ALCOHOL.

"THAT WASN'T AS BAD AS I WAS THINKING IT
WOULD BE. ALL THINGS CONSIDERED," SHE
SAID.
HE LIFTED HIS EYES AND GAVE HER A LOOK
AS THOUGH QUESTIONING HER SANITY.
"OH, I DON'T MEAN THE STRIGA AND ALL

THAT," SHE SAID. "I MEAN THE BLOOD DRINKING THING. I DON'T KNOW WHY YOU WERE SO WORRIED ABOUT TELLING ME THAT."

"WELL, MOST NORMAL PEOPLE ARE A LITTLE SHY ABOUT DRINKING BLOOD," HE SAID SETTING THE SWAB ASIDE AND FITTING A BAND-AID OVER HER WRIST. "IT'S A THING I'M TOLD."

"WELL, I GUESS I'M NOT NORMAL THEN," SHE SAID WITH A SMILE.

"I COULD'VE TOLD YOU THAT," HE SAID.

SHE SWATTED HIM PLAYFULLY.

"EITHER THAT," SHE CONTINUED. "OR, I LOVE YOU ENOUGH TO STOMACH THE IDEA OF DRINKING YOUR BLOOD."
HE LOOKED UP AT HER A SMILE SPREADING ACROSS HIS FACE AS THOUGH HE WAS ONLY JUST BEGINNING TO REGISTER WHAT SHE'D SAID.

"IF...IF THAT'S THE CASE," HE SAID. "THEN, I GUESS I LOVE YOU ENOUGH NOT TO DRINK TOO MUCH OF YOUR BLOOD."

NOW IT WAS HER TURN TO SMILE AS HER HEART BEGAN TO DANCE JUST A BIT IN HER CHEST.

"IF THAT'S NOT LOVE," SHE SAID. "I DON'T KNOW WHAT IS."

STILL SMILING AS WIDELY AS HE COULD, HE LIFTED HER WRIST TO HIS LIPS AND KISSED THE BAND-AID GENTLY, GRAY EYES NEVER LEAVING HERS.

SHE OPENED HER PALM AND, JUST AS GENTLY, BROUGHT HIS LIPS TO MEET WITH HERS. SHE FELT HIS DESIRE, MIXED WITH A WELL-FASHIONED RESTRAINT. THAT HINT OF RESTRAINT, SHE KNEW, WOULD ALWAYS BE THERE. IT WOULD KEEP HER...THEM...SAFE.

AND THAT, TRULY, WAS LOVE.

Printed by BoD˜in Norderstedt, Germany

9 789657 775745